CINDERELLA MAN

THE SHOOTING SCRIPT

CINDERELLA MAN

SCREENPLAY BY ~~WITHDRAWN~~
CLIFF HOLLINGSWORTH AND AKIVA GOLDSMAN

STORY BY CLIFF HOLLINGSWORTH

INTRODUCTIONS BY RON HOWARD, BRIAN GRAZER,
CLIFF HOLLINGSWORTH, AND AKIVA GOLDSMAN

A Newmarket Shooting Script® Series Book
NEWMARKET PRESS • NEW YORK

The Newmarket Shooting Script® Series is a registered trademark of
Newmarket Publishing & Communications Company.

This book is published simultaneously in the United States of America and in Canada.

FIRST EDITION

10 9 8 7 6 5 4 3 2 1

ISBN: 1-55704-651-4

Library of Congress Catalog-in-Publication Data available upon request.

QUANTITY PURCHASES

Companies, professional groups, clubs, and other organizations may qualify for special terms when ordering quantities
of this title. For information, write to Special Sales, Newmarket Press, 18 East 48th Street, New York, NY 10017;
call (212) 832-3575 or 1-800-669-3903; FAX (212) 832-3629; or e-mail info@newmarketpress.com.

Website: www.newmarketpress.com

Manufactured in the United States of America.

Acknowledgment of Permissions
We gratefully acknowledge permission to reprint the following copyrighted material:
Page 145: *Relief to Royalty* excerpt courtesy of *The Hudson Dispatch*. p. 149: "Knockout Predicted by Baer" © 1935,
2005 by the New York Times Co. Reprinted with permission. p. 151: "Braddock Outpoints Baer to Win World Title"
© 1935, 2005 by the New York Times Co. Reprinted with permission. p. 152: "Mrs. Braddock Weeps Happily on
Hearing Decision Over Radio" © 1935, 2005 by the New York Times Co. Reprinted with permission. p. 154: "Baer's
Hands Broken…" courtesy of *The New York Post*. p. 156: "In His Own Words" excerpt from *In This Corner*, by Peter
Heller, courtesy of Simon & Schuster; p. 159: "Braddock, Who Beat Baer for Title, Dies" © 1974, 2005 by the New
York Times Co. Reprinted with permission. Photos on pages 145, 148, 150, 153, and 161 © Bettmann/Corbis.
The publisher has made every effort to contact copyright holders; any errors or omissions are inadvertent and will be
corrected upon notice in future reprintings.

CONTENTS

Russell Crowe, Brian Grazer, his daughter Sage Grazer, and Ron Howard

INTRODUCTIONS

BY RON HOWARD

As a filmmaker (and moviegoer), I find nothing more interesting than a character embarking on a compelling journey. It can be as fundamental as a father trying to define his role in an extended family, or as sweeping as a crew of astronauts attempting to return from the moon. Whatever the character's course, what I find most intriguing, most revealing are the moments during the struggle—when they have no idea whether or not they will even succeed. We as an audience may have a good idea what the outcome will be, but the characters onscreen are simply trying to cope in the situation, to reach for that goal. And it is exactly those character-defining moments that tell us who this person really is, and that is what draws me as a filmmaker to a project.

It is most telling to me that James Braddock did not enter the boxing ring with a champion title on his mind. He stepped between the ropes with a much simpler goal, a selfless one in fact. As the hardships the nation faced grew more dire, the crucible of the times reduced dreams to their most basic. Here was a man trying to keep his family together, fed and sheltered during that dark period called the Great Depression. Boxing was the best way he knew how to do that. Just as much as moving loads on a dock, boxing was his job.

Although Braddock became a hero to the nation, he was always heroic in the eyes of his family. His story continues to be so incredibly stirring because it is a tale that reminds us just how remarkable human endurance and the power of love can be.

I did not come to the Braddock story with a clean slate. While growing up, my father had regaled me with stories about the Braddock-Baer fight, which was the first fight he remembers hearing. He was about seven or eight at the time, huddled around a pool hall radio with his father, who had driven him into town expressly for that purpose. My dad would always tell the story of Jim Braddock as an example of courage, personal integrity, and the willing of oneself to do something not just for personal gain, but to do right by the people around you.

Just as Braddock drew strength from his family, urging him forward, I was able to present Braddock's story for the screen because of the tireless effort and immeasurable contributions of a number of incredibly gifted people. Cliff Hollingsworth's many years of work brought Braddock's life out of the dimness of nearly forgotten history and presented us with a shaking tale. Akiva Goldsman's mastery of screenwriting burnished and strengthened the script. Akiva, honestly no particular fan of boxing, was, however, an absolute believer in the power of this uniquely human survival story. He took advantage of additional research into the lives of the Braddocks, and ultimately lost himself in the emotional struggle of this family and wrote his way out, creating on the page even more rich opportunities for the extraordinary cast and all of us behind the camera to sink our creative teeth into. Russell Crowe's devotion to the project brought it to my attention and his unmatchable ability to remake himself brought Braddock to towering, rich, complex, seamless, astounding life; not only did he mentally throw himself into the role, he literally put himself in harm's way during the boxing sequences—returning to filming a mere five weeks after shoulder surgery—to physically portray Braddock. Renée Zellweger's passion for this story fueled a quiet creative intensity that not only breathed truth and life into Mae, but inspired us all every day she filmed.

Paul Giamatti's jewel-maker ability renders the character of Joe Gould immense and masterfully detailed. Stacey Snider's commitment and tremendous leadership involving *Cinderella Man* spanned years and never flagged. Thank you, Stacey. Also my thanks must be extended for the countless contributions from a score of talented actors and accomplished filmmakers. And certainly I owe Brian Grazer, my friend, business partner, and a superlative filmmaker, my usual huge debt for bringing this "family" together with true vision so we could tell the Braddocks' remarkable story.

There is something inherently tough about Americans. They will not admit defeat. Failure is not an option. The astronauts of Apollo 13 would not give up. John and Alicia Nash would not give up. And Jim Braddock would not surrender to poverty. As moving and inspiring as Jim Braddock's story is on the outside, it's only when you get on the inside—inside his love for his wife and the simple desire to take care of his family—that you see the real basis for his courage which makes his story so powerful and enduringly relevant.

Cinderella Man is not the story of a great boxer. It is the story of a great man. That's the heart and soul of the movie.

BY BRIAN GRAZER

When Russell Crowe recounted the story of Jim Braddock to me, I found it so heartbreaking and emotional. And since it spoke so strongly to me, I had that filmmaker's hunch that it would speak to other people, too.

I guess what had moved me so about Braddock was the simplicity of the story, its universality. So much of its power lies in the fact that is it relatable. Sure, you might not have suffered through the Depression (although someone in your family most probably did), and you might not have had a shot at being world champion of anything. But, in the simple living of life, you've faced something you felt was insurmountable and yet, because of the high stakes involved, you gave it your best shot. Maybe you overcame it, maybe you didn't. But you know that situation and the feelings associated with that...and you therefore know a little something about what motivated Jim Braddock.

His is the story of a regular guy who faced the hardest of times with remarkable courage. To me, it's a story about all of us and about the hardship America has experienced in its young history. Here you have this man who didn't have money to feed his kids, who had a broken hand, who was never supposed to box again, and he goes on to become the champion of the world, to achieve a greatness no one ever saw coming. That's an amazing fable, even though it's entirely true. You might call it a classic American story.

Ron Howard is an extraordinarily skilled filmmaker, but what differentiates him from other filmmakers is his approach to American themes. His movies form a sort of American nucleus. They tell stories that sound quite simple. Of course, anything that sounds simple always ends up to be anything but. The circumstances under which his stories unfold render them complex trials for those involved—coming home is simple, but try coming home from the moon. Feeding your family can be simple, only strive to do it when there's precious little for anyone anywhere to eat.

One could call Braddock and his story "simple" in a way. He was a kind and generous man. Straightforward. He had a lot of humility and that was something that everybody could grab ahold of and see a little part of themselves in him. In that way, he was almost more of a champion outside of the ring than he was in it. His is really a story of everyday heroism.

That said, Jim Braddock had no eccentricities—as a character, he comes with few interesting or dynamic personality hooks. He wasn't the funniest guy in the room. He didn't have an inner life that was dark. He didn't have those complexities. The good news is that there is tremendous simplicity to the story. But for a filmmaker, that can also be the bad news, because it is hard to make a movie without speed bumps or complications that set the audience off balance. Yet Ron handles this gracefully. I think living inside the epicenter of this fairy tale enabled him to find the perfect little details that make the story unpredictable and yet still lead us to a place that is emotionally conclusive. Couple that with Russell's portrayal of Braddock—a layered, powerful, and loving man—and the story becomes not only unique, but also universal. Simple, yes, but far from simplistic. I've never seen anyone dedicate themselves to a part with more intensity than Russell Crowe, nor anyone better able to spin a compelling, moving story than Ron Howard.

I think what Ron and I have found is that there's some sort of alchemy in this friendship that we have, and within that alchemy there is a letter in our DNA that simply says: tell stories. And that's the thing that we have together—the need to tell our stories on film.

BY CLIFF HOLLINGSWORTH

Michael Brown, University of South Carolina Publications

The journey began in 1994 when I happened to think about Jim Braddock, "The Cinderella Man," and his incredible rags to riches story. I thought about what a great movie the Braddock story would make.

I was already familiar with the story. As a long time boxing fan, I'd read about all of the former heavyweight champions. Jim Braddock has always been my favorite.

I became even more convinced that this could make a great movie after telling the story to Abraham Gordon. Both he and his wife, Jodi, are friends and sounding boards and Abraham is a creative genius. At the time, he was the Director of Development at Spectacor Films. They produced low-budget movies, so a big-budget period piece was not for them. I remember Abraham's reaction to the story. He said, "If you write that, you're looking at one great movie." We both saw it not as a boxing story but as a story about the triumph of the human spirit.

At the time, I was an unknown, unproduced aspiring writer who was working as a substitute teacher and dividing my time between California and South Carolina because of my mother's health.

I was represented by Ed McCormick and Irby Walker, both in South Carolina. My brother, Mike, also worked as my agent.

The idea of getting a big-budget period piece to the screen about a largely forgotten boxer from the 1930s by an unproduced writer with unknown representation faced some odds.

Then I got a lucky break. I was able to track down Joe Mallon, a nephew of Jim Braddock, who put me in touch with Braddock's two sons, Jay and Howard. After meeting Jay, he and Howard agreed to cooperate with me.

At this point, let me express my everlasting appreciation to Jay and Howard Braddock. They couldn't have been more supportive. Jim Braddock must have been a great father. He raised two sons to be outstanding men. Jay, in particular, was an invaluable research source and Joe Mallon had a scrapbook covering Braddock's whole career. I'm very appreciative to Joe, also.

Sadly, Jay died three years ago and won't get to see the movie about his father. But what a good friend and tremendous help he was.

I wrote the screenplay and went forward with it in 1996. My friend, Abraham, made a few attempts to get me a bigger agent but no one would even read my script.

So I went forward with Ed, Irby, and my brother, Mike. It was Mike who pitched the story to Andrea Asimow of Penny Marshall's company, Parkway. She agreed to accept the script. I know now that the script went home that weekend with 40 other scripts with a female reader who hates boxing. Yet, she recommended *Cinderella Man*. So did Andrea to Penny Marshall, who loved it. Penny sent it to Universal and they wanted it.

Mike had also gotten it to Turner Pictures and they wanted it. Abraham had predicted that if anyone read the script, they would want to get involved.

I optioned the script to Universal. It had a couple of false starts. It looked like the second option would expire and I'd get the rights back. Interested parties were waiting and Abraham had lined up a very lucrative offer. But at the last minute, Miramax got involved and now the movie has been made, a co-production of Universal and Miramax.

The Jim Braddock story is unusual in more ways than one. He inspired the nation in 1935 and was a national hero. Yet, he became a largely forgotten figure. Jay told me of how he would mention that his father was once the heavyweight champion of the world and usually the person would never have heard of Jim Braddock. That was very frustrating for Jay. I've encountered the same reaction continuously. Most people don't know who he was. But that will soon change and this forgotten hero will be remembered once again, this time, hopefully, forever through the power of a movie.

I'm glad that I played a part. And it has been a long ride.

BY AKIVA GOLDSMAN

To tell the story of Jim Braddock was an extraordinary opportunity for me. Here was the amazing architecture of a man's life, existing against the backdrop of one of the darkest periods of our country's history. Stories like these, so difficult for those who live them, are gifts to writers. The universe offers them up and I think it is our luxury as well as our obligation to return them in some emotionally understandable form.

Braddock's story is famously uplifting. The title of the movie itself, arguably, makes the outcome clear. All fairy tales end happily ever after. But lives do not have titles. They are not seen through the lens of happy endings but are instead a roiling sea of unpredictability, profound sorrow, heart-rending joy. If Jim's story was God-given, full of grace, the experience of his life needed to be rendered as the opposite. We set out to create a narrative that was blind to future outcomes, one that remembers just how unimaginable the prospect of triumph is before it arrives.

In screenwriting, the old adage applies: Story *is* character. So there's an old screenwriter's trick often used to shape narrative. You've got about two hours. You know character is best revealed in conflict. So you build your screenplay around conflict. Not just any conflict will do, mind you. You need a singular episode where your main character—this part is important—where he or she is in conflict with him- (or her-) *self.* Mid-life crisis, crisis of faith, crisis of conscience, crisis of love, any moment where one must rise up over one's darker side is just fine. In this regard Jim Braddock presented only one small problem. He didn't have a dark side.

Jim Braddock was a fundamentally decent man. His attachment to his family was profound. His ability to withstand hardship was truly inspirational. The crises he faced were less ones of internal conflict than those of circumstance. Jim was born into a failing world. His greatest gift, perhaps, was to not falter, despite an entirely unyielding time.

So, the terrible news for Jim was the good news for his story; despite how hard he tried, the world kept getting worse. We focused the script on his seemingly never-ending string of bad times; there's hardly a scene between the fights where something awful doesn't happen. We drew the world with real darkness in order to better reveal Jim's light.

We believed that happily-ever-afters do exist. But that getting to them can be pretty awful. We believed that fairy tales are probably no fun at all for those who live inside them. So we set out to tell our story just that way, all in hopes of making Jim's triumph at the end all the sweeter.

I hope we succeeded.

Once again, this movie allowed me to continue my collaboration with Brian Grazer, Ron Howard, and Russell Crowe. Of all the jobs I have, this one is my very favorite. We have a shorthand with each other, a daily routine, before and during shooting, to dig deeper, turn the scene upside down, right it again. These men make my work far better than it has any right to be. I go to school watching Ron draw on film the smallest of emotions and the sharpest of ideas. I am stilled to awe by Russell's refined force, his impossible truthfulness in transformation. And we have good fun together, too.

I am grateful to our new partners on this project, the insanely talented Paul Giamatti and the simply perfect Renée Zellweger—grateful for their words, their hearts, their talent.

The Braddocks lived this difficult life and, by their suffering, made our nation a little bit better. Cliff Hollingsworth excavated the bones of this tale, painstakingly restored them and unveiled them for the world to see. He championed the Braddocks' story and saw, before any of us, the power and importance of their saga.

As this is, at its heart, a love story, I'd like to acknowledge the women in my life. So thanks again to my two mothers, Mira Rothenberg and Elizabeth Lee who themselves lived through these troubled times.

And I dedicate this to my wife, Rebecca. Because it turns out everybody gets one Cinderella Story in their lifetime. And she is mine.

CINDERELLA MAN

Screenplay by

Cliff Hollingsworth and Akiva Goldsman

Story by

Cliff Hollingsworth

Final draft
August 24,2004

1   FADE IN ON: 1

A BACK AND WHITE IMAGE-CLOSE. Of a FIGHTER being HIT, jaw
distending too far, an impossible angle. Time stands still.

Color BLEEDS into the image. Time returns. The punch
FINISHES, mighty, moving shoulders obscuring a storm of
blows. That FIGHTER falls amidst a DIN of YELLS and CHEERS.

                    ANNOUNCER (OVER)
              And from the great state of New
              Jersey, by technical knockout,
              tonight's light heavyweight
              winner...Jim Braddock.

2   INT. MADISON SQUARE GARDEN - NYC - 1928 - NIGHT   2

The capacity crowd is on its feet. That WINNER with his fist
in the air is wiry, not too tall, not too heavy. The kind of
fighter you'd say had a lot of heart. Meet JIM BRADDOCK.

A little GUY rushes in from the corner of the ring, drenched
in sweat, bright, intelligent eyes. By the looks of him, he
may have just fought this fight himself. This is JOE GOULD
and he actually leaps onto Braddock's back like a kid.

People are on their feet, SCREAMING, YELLING. Affluent faces
out for a night. A world, happy, with no knowledge of the
future. It's still the roaring twenties, after all.

Gould shoots Jim a wry smile. Braddock grins back. Pumps his
fist in the air and, on cue, the crowd goes WILD.

3   EXT. MADISON SQUARE GARDEN - NYC - NIGHT   3

New York sparkled then. A world of black shadows, and clear
white light. Simpler times.

Joe and Jim emerge from the side door under a huge lighted
sign for tonight's fight, face those hungry for autographs.

                    JOE
              Just give a few, leave em wanting.

They have stopped before a WOMAN waiting with a program.

                    BRADDOCK
              You want to sign my name for me
              too?

                    JOE
              Least then they could read it.

                    BRADDOCK
          Hand it to skill and experience
          over here.

The Woman looks bewildered. Jim smiles, takes the program.

                    BRADDOCK
          Better let me.
               (conspiratorial)
          Not so sure he can spell.

Jim signs away. Glossies of him in a staged boxer pose.
Naturalism is still two wars off.

                    FAN
          Gave him a cold meat party, Jim.

                    FAN # 2
          Way to go, Braddock.

Jim likes these guys, the fact that they love him so. A GIRL
catches his eye, flashes him, underneath her flapper's dress,
a glimpse of naked promise. Jim smiles, shakes his head.

                    JOE
          Hey, win some, lose some, huh
          Johnston?

Jim looks up to see two other MEN leaving from the smoky side
door. The fellow Joe is addressing is JIMMY JOHNSTON. Fight
promoter. Johnston doesn't look happy.

                    BRADDOCK
          Leave it be, Joe.

Joe nods as if he agrees. It's just that he has absolutely no
control over his mouth.

                    JOE
          Although you gotta figure, this
          one, you gotta figure maybe you get
          behind the wrong guys. What's
          Griffith favored, six to one and,
          oh yeah, outweighs my boy by, what,
          five pounds more than that scale
          you fixed says, then jab, cross...

Joe is actually moving in time with the hits. Now that Joe's
started, Jim can't leave him out there on his own.

                    BRADDOCK
          Actually it was jab, **jab,** cross-

                    JOE
          Jab, jab, cross and your boy's
          hearing high ball whistles. Hell, I
          could hear em. You Jimmy?

                    BRADDOCK
          I heard something.

                    JOE
          So maybe no one's a bum after all,
          huh Johnston...?

Johnston just holds Joe's eyes. The beat lasts. Then he turns
and walks to his waiting car. Joe smiles.

                    JOE
          TKO.

                    BRADDOCK
          I won on a knockout, Joe.

Joe smiles.

                    JOE
          Not you. Me.

                    BRADDOCK
          I'll get a cab.

                    JOE
          A cab? **James?**

Joe gestures to the curb where a limo waits. Eyes sparkle.

                    JOE
          Jimmy, we gotta talk.

4   INT. LIMO - MOVING   4

See the passing city through the windows. Almost no one
remembers it this way anymore. Life as a dream.

                    JOE
          So I'm saying it.

                    BRADDOCK
          No you don't. You'll jinx it.

Braddock watches as Joe pours scotch from a brown-bagged
fifth in silence.

                              JOE
                    That's ten in a row. Ten in a
                    goddamn row.

Braddock LAUGHS.

                              JOE
                    What?

                              BRADDOCK
                    Just seeing how long you could stay
                    quiet is all.

Joe shoots him a look, continues.

                              JOE
                    You're getting stronger every
                    fight, I been seeing it.

                              BRADDOCK
                    So you're not blind, after all.

                              JOE
                    You may favor the right, sure, but
                    you got no stage fright or nerves.
                    And you never been knocked out.

Something more focused about their fun. A seriousness to it.

                              JOE
                    You're in line now, Jimmy. You're
                    gonna get your shot.

Jim nods, smiles, knows it's true. They ride on. Two kids in
a big car, drinking scotch and smoking big cigars.

                              JOE
                    We need to get you out being seen.
                    Flash-flash, bing-bing. Satchmo's
                    playing the Savoy. And there's this
                    new jinny uptown.

Jim just looks at him, a simple smile in his eyes.

                              BRADDOCK
                    Home, Joe.

Joe's protest doesn't get past his lips.

                              BRADDOCK
                    Home.

Joe shakes his head in familiar resignation.

                    JOE
               (to the driver)
          Jersey, Frank. For Mr. Adventure.

Joe is already into his pocket pulling out a wad of cash.
Starts peeling off bills.

                    JOE
          Here's $886 for Jeannette and $264
          each for the two bucket kids, $300
          for the ring fees, my $2658 and
          your $3244 makes $8860.

He hands Jim the remaining cash.

                    BRADDOCK
          You could come in for a drink? The
          kids would love to see you.

                    JOE
          You still married to the same girl?

                    BRADDOCK
          I was this morning.

                    JOE
          Maybe a rain check. And tell her I
          undercharged on the Gym fees and no
          load on the towels, would ya?

                    BRADDOCK
          I'll point it out.

5   EXT. BRADDOCK HOUSE - NEWARK - NIGHT   5

A lovely white colonial sits on a tree-lined street. Jim
watches the limo pull off, then turns to the house as the
front door swings open.

Framed in the glow of hall light is a WOMAN too lovely to be
any man's wife. MAE BRADDOCK.

She looks at him, eyes flooded with relief at the sight of
him before they ask the question she won't give voice. Jim
looks down, the slightest shake of his head.

What flashes in her eyes for a second is almost resignation,
a knowing that this day must inevitably come.

But when Mae looks up again Jim is smiling, this small
practical joke passed as she rushes into his arms.

                          MAE
                    (soft, in his ear)
               I could kill you.

Doesn't sound like killing's what she's talking about.

                       BRADDOCK
               I like the sound of that.

Jim is already kissing her, hands moving over her body.

                          MAE
               Jimmy, my **sister**.

Jim looks at the door where a slightly older woman, ALICE,
has emerged into the hall light. Two small BOYS (JAY, 4,
HOWARD, 3) race out into the street past her.

                          JAY
               Daddy, did you win?

Jim lifts one by the belt for his kiss, leans down to kiss
the older one's head.

6   EXT. GARDEN - NIGHT   6

Mae and Jim sit at a table in the backyard. Empty wine bottle
and burned down candles. Mae is tipsy.

                          MAE
               Was he a real slugger?

                       BRADDOCK
               You could come watch.

Something flashes in her averting eyes. Fear?

                          MAE
               You get punched, every time, it
               feels like I'm getting punched too.
               And I ain't half as tough as you.

But as she looks back to him, the fear is hidden by a smile.

                          MAE
               And who wants those articles about
               me running out on a fight again?

He takes her hands, kisses her knuckles.

                          MAE
               Tell me about the girls.

                    BRADDOCK
          Were there girls?

                    MAE
          Come on. There was one.

                    BRADDOCK
          Yeah. Maybe there was one.

Familiar game.

                    MAE
          Blond?

                    BRADDOCK
          A brunette.

                    MAE
          Tall?

                    BRADDOCK
          Like a gazelle. Don't know how she
          breathed up there.

Mae rises, moving around Jim.

                    MAE
          Oh, Mr. Braddock. You're so strong.

Head bowed.

                    MAE
          Your hands are so big.

Eyes up and batting.

                    MAE
          So powerful.

She moves in close, her VOICE suddenly sincere.

                    MAE
          I'm so proud of you, Jimmy.

Mae begins climbing on Jim's lap.

                    MAE
          Introducing two time state golden
          gloves title holder...

Up onto his knees.

                    MAE
          ...In Both the light heavyweight
          and heavyweight divisions...

Now standing on his thighs.

                    MAE
          21 and 0 with 16 wins coming by way
          of knockout...

Holding his eyes.

                    MAE
          ...The Bulldog of Bergen, the Pride
          of New Jersey, and the hope of the
          Irish as future champion of the
          world...
               (shouting)
          James J. Braddock!

He rises, lifting her up, her hands already under his shirt
kissing now, as they move into the cool cover of shadow.

7   INT. BRADDOCK HOUSE - BEDROOM - NIGHT   7

Richly furnished. Jim stands undressing as (OVER) he can hear
Mae WHISPERING to the children in the room next door.

Jim takes off his watch and lays it on the bureau beside a
silver framed wedding picture. Then he takes a gold cross off
his neck, kisses it, lays it down as well.

HOLD on the face of a man who knows for a second the good
luck of this moment, his life. CAMERA begins to circle him.

CAMERA comes around his back as years fall away in passing
dark, CAMERA coming back around to find a bureau top with no
watch, no cross, that wedding picture now without its frame.

JIM-OLDER. Nose broken. Ear gone cauliflower. Face shadowed
by a morning beard and hard days beyond youth's imagining.
WIDER...

8   INT. BRADDOCK BASEMENT APARTMENT - BEDROOM - 1933 - 4:00AM 8

Jim stands dressing at the bureau. Far smaller than the room
we were just in. All the beautiful furniture is long gone.
Partitioned by a hanging blanket beyond which bulb light
shines. In bed, now THREE KIDS sleep, (ROSEMARIE, 6, Howard,
8, Jay, 10) Jim pushes through the blanket into...

INT. BRADDOCK APARTMENT - KITCHEN - CONTINUOUS

The other side of this two room apartment. A kitchen with a
table and a sofa not far off make up the rest of their home.

Jim crosses to Mae who stands over an old gas stove frying
two thin slices of bologna. In the naked light we see Jim is
thinner than before, dark circles around his eyes.

                    BRADDOCK
          Can't find my good socks.

                    MAE
               (turning)
          Jim!

Her VOICE is a scolding WHISPER.

                    BRADDOCK
               (now whispering too)
          Sorry. God. Sorry.

But the damage is done. Stirring from the other room.

                    ROSEMARIE (OVER)
               (sleepy whimper)
          ...Mama.

                    MAE
          Great.

Mae takes Jim's socks out of the oven.

                    BRADDOCK
          Sorry.

She shakes her head at him with resignation, already slicing
a third slice of meat from the meager stump.

                    MAE
          I washed them last night. I took
          them right off your feet, remember?

Jim just shakes his head.

                    MAE
          You were dead to the world.

Jim sits at the table, pulling on those socks.

                    BRADDOCK
          How can I keep em this warm?

A little figure wanders out. Rosemarie.

                    ROSEMARIE
          Mama, I want to eat too.

She climbs up on Jim's lap without a word. He reflexively
smooths her hair, smells her head, eyes closed. Mae watches.

                    MAE
          We got a notice yesterday. On the
          gas and electric.

Jim reaches behind her, sets a mason jar on the kitchen
table. Only a few coins.

                    BRADDOCK
          It must have been raining more
          lately than I noticed.

Jim sets his daughter on a chair.

                    BRADDOCK
          I'll get the milk.

10   EXT. BRADDOCK APARTMENT - PRE DAWN   10

Jim emerges into the tenement courtyard. A long way from his
tree lined street. He walks to the sooty basement window in
meager light. Something skitters past. A rat. Jim ignores it.

Jim reaches down and lifts two milk bottles in his hands.
Both empty. Each wears a pink past due slip like a collar.

11   INT. BRADDOCK APARTMENT - MOMENTS LATER   11

Jim ENTERS and wordlessly sets the bottles atop the fridge.
Mae hold his eyes. In his averted glance, shame.

                    MAE
          Oh. Some left over, I think.

Mae finds a last cold bottle, maybe an eighth full. She
begins topping it off with water.

                    MAE
          Who needs a cow?

Mae slides the crackling meat onto plates, lays one down in
front of each of them.

                    BRADDOCK
          Rosy. Your fork, please.

Little one reluctantly obeys.

                  BRADDOCK
        I got Feldman tonight. That's half
        a C. I beat him, maybe I can get
        back up to seventy five.

Mae looks up at him. That old fear in her eyes better hidden
than the doubt in his.

                  ROSEMARIE
      Mama, I want some more.

                  MAE
        I'm sorry, honey. We need to save
        some for the boys.

Rosemarie has finished her bologna, as has Mae. Jim's still
sits on his plate.

                  BRADDOCK
        Mae, you know what I dreamed about
        last night. I dreamed I was having
        dinner at the Ritz and I had a big
        thick, steak...

He has risen, is putting on coat, gloves, hat.

                  BRADDOCK
        This thick, Rosy, and so much
        mashed potatoes and ice cream, I'm
        just not hungry, anymore.

Rosemarie stares up at him skeptically.

                  BRADDOCK
        Can you help me out? Mommy cooked
        and I don't want it to go to waste.

Jim deposits his bologna on his daughter's plate.

                  MAE
      Jimmy-

But he stills his wife's protest with a kiss.

                  BRADDOCK
      You're my girls.

Mae watches Rosemarie devour the meat hungrily as Jim goes,
an impossible mix of emotions in her eyes.

12   EXT. NEWARK - 1933 - 4:30 AM - THE GREAT DEPRESSION   12

Jim passes an abandoned lot lit by trash can fires where several cars idle, windows steamed opaque with breath.

One car door opens, a MOTHER pushing out two KIDS who stumble out, bleary eyed, and pee against the wall.

Jim walks on. Stores are boarded up.

Men walk the streets in suits and ties, like ghosts, nowhere to go. Others sit on benches, bus stops, heads bowed.

13   EXT. LOADING DOCK - EARLY MORNING   13

Jim and 60 other DESPERATE MEN crowd the gate of a long chain-link fence. Dawn hits the Hudson and Manhattan beyond.

A middle-aged FOREMAN, JAKE emerges through the gate with a clipboard in hand, stares at faces stoned by sleeplessness.

> JAKE
> I need nine men and nine men only.

Jim jostles, trying to be seen. Jake begins pointing out the lucky ones, joyless in his power over life and death.

> JAKE
> Six, seven, eight...

Jim's gotten there early enough to be at the front of the pack but there are still far too many men than are needed.

> JAKE
> Nine.

Jim's not among the chosen. A MAN (BEN) SHOUTS.

> BEN
> I been here since four.

> JAKE
> Sorry brother, luck of the draw.

Most are already heading off to look elsewhere. That's when Ben actually pulls a gun, points it at Jake's chest.

> BEN
> I was here first.
> (hand shaking)
> What about it?

Jake stares at the gun a beat, clearly rattled. Looks back up at the man. Time has gone perfectly still.

> JAKE
> My mistake, pal. I need ten.

Ben crosses through the gate. He's barely put the gun away when a few of the guys jump him, wrestle him to the ground.

Jim stares down at his feet, beneath his ratty shoes a newspaper head reads: UNEMPLOYED REACHES 15,000,000.

14   EXT. BRADDOCK APARTMENT - DAY   14

Jim returns home to find Howard jumping on a mattress spring out on the fire escape landing overhead.

> HOWARD
> (looking down)
> No shifts today, dad?

But Jim's easy smile seems to say, win some, lose some.

> BRADDOCK
> What you doing, son?

> HOWARD
> I'm being good. I'm being quiet.
> I'm being *hayve*.

> BRADDOCK
> ...Good?

That's when Rosy comes racing from down the ally.

> ROSEMARIE
> Daddy, Daddy, Daddy!

She catapults into his arms.

> BRADDOCK
> What sweetheart?

She grins at him like neon.

> ROSEMARIE
> Jay **stole**!

15   INT. BRADDOCK HOUSE - DAY   15

Jim ENTERS to find Mae standing over Jay, boy's face shut tight, facing the floor. He sets Rosy down.

                    BRADDOCK
          What's this all about?

                    ROSY
          See. It's a salami.

Mae looks up sharply at her daughter.

                    MAE
          Your brother is in enough trouble
          without you telling, young lady.

Mae gestures to the hard salami on the table.

                    MAE
          From the butcher's. He won't say a
          word about it, will you Jay?

Mae hold's Jim's eyes. A silent hand-off.

                    BRADDOCK
          Okay. Pick it up. Let's go.

Jay looks up at his father.

                    BRADDOCK
          Right now!

Jim has already re-opened the front door.

16   EXT. BUTCHER'S SHOP - DAY   16

Through the window, Jay is handing the salami back to the
butcher (SAM) who nods, returning it to the case.

The two Braddocks emerge, start down the street. Jim says
nothing, knows his quiet son, waits as they continue on.

                    JAY
               (finally)
          Marty Johnson had to go away to
          Delaware and live with his uncle.

Jim still says nothing.

                    JAY
          His parents didn't have enough
          money for them to eat.

Jim stops, turns to face his son.

                    BRADDOCK
          You got scared and I can understand
          it.

He holds his son's eyes.

                    BRADDOCK
          But we don't steal. No matter what
          happens. Not ever. Got me?

Jay manages a nod.

                    BRADDOCK
          Are you giving me your word?

                    JAY
          Yes.

                    BRADDOCK
          Go on.

                    JAY
          I promise.

                    BRADDOCK
          Things aren't so good right now,
          Jay, you're right. But Daddy's
          doing his best.

He touches his son's cheek.

                    BRADDOCK
          There's a lot of other people a lot
          less fortunate than us. And if you
          take something somebody else goes
          without.

Jim goes down on his haunches. Looks at his boy, eye to eye.

                    BRADDOCK
          Here's my word, good as wheat in
          the bin. We're never going to send
          you away, son.

See Jay's small lips already trembling.

                    BRADDOCK
          I promise.

And finally the tears come, spilling from Jay's eyes, Jim
wrapping his son tight in his arms and holding him close.

17   INT. LOCKER ROOM - NIGHT   17

Low rent. Joe stands in front of Jim, taping up his hands.
Joe's clothes still show smart indications of wealth.

>   JOE
>   He's a slow guy. He plants himself.
>   Keep him in the middle. And dance
>   around him. You know what to do.
>   Guy's a bum.

>   BRADDOCK
>   I know two bits will buy a guy a
>   seat, a guy who gets to watch you
>   bleed and call you a bum. I know
>   because he's a paying customer I
>   have to take it from him.

>   JOE
>   I see. Well. Pardon me. Let me
>   restate. Mr. Abraham Feldman is a
>   novice fighter whose ass you should
>   gently kick until it is humped up
>   between his shoulders. That is, of
>   course, if it doesn't offend your
>   overly sensitive nature.

Joe switches hands. Jim winces. Joe looks down.

>   JOE
>   This break's still a couple weeks
>   away. Why didn't you tell me, Jim?

>   BRADDOCK
>   Can't get any shifts. We owe
>   everybody.

>   JOE
>   Screw it. I'll tape it double.

Joe shakes his head, commences the illegal double taping.

>   JOE
>   So, this extraordinary opponent of
>   yours who my grandma could beat,
>   with her breath, you keep your left
>   in his face and when his head pops
>   up like a little bunny rabbit boom.
>   One shot. Make it good. Finish
>   early, I'll buy you an egg cream.

18   INT. MOUNT VERNON ARMORY BOXING RING - FIGHT NIGHT   18

Smaller. A CROWD beyond the ring lights is a sea of hats
floating on smoking heads. Faces are gaunter, more desperate.

The ring is circled with JUDGES, GAMBLERS, HOTTIES,
REPORTERS. PHOTOGRAPHERS sit with flashbulbs ready to sizzle.

>   RADIO COMMENTATOR (V.O.)
>   Jim Braddock, just five years ago,
>   was considered first in line for
>   the world championship. But in the
>   last year he's lost ten fights and
>   hasn't managed a single kayo.

Jim crawls under the rope. Jim shadow boxes in his corner as
Joe massages his shoulder.

The crowd yells and stamps as ABE FELDMAN makes his way down
a crowded aisle toward the ring.

>   RADIO COMMENTATOR (V.O.) (CONT'D)
>   Now Braddock faces Abe Feldman, an
>   up-and-comer with seventeen wins,
>   one draw and one loss. In less than
>   two years he has recorded nine
>   kayos.

Jim tenses and Joe feels it in Jim's shoulders.

>   JOE
>   Who whipped Latzo?

>   BRADDOCK
>   (softly)
>   I did.

>   JOE
>   Who k.o.'d Slattery in the 9th when
>   everybody said he didn't have a
>   Rainmaker's chance in hell?!

His answer is barely audible. Little enthusiasm.

>   BRADDOCK
>   I did.

>   JOE
>   That's right. But we should pucker
>   our assholes over Feldman?

>   BRADDOCK
>   No.

The crowd ROARS as Feldman climbs into the ring. Joe's TONE
grows sharp, angry.

> JOE
> Jimmy, Jimmy, look at me! Is there
> someplace else you'd rather be?

> BRADDOCK
> No.

> JOE
> Good. So what are you going to do?

When Jim's words come, they are soft and lethal.

> BRADDOCK
> I'm gonna get an egg cream.

> JOE
> There you go. That's the spirit.

19   INT. MOUNT VERNON ARMORY BOXING RING - MINUTES LATER   19

Jim takes a hard punch to the face, going backwards. Jim
moves in but Feldman is blocking his drive.

20   INT. THE CORNER   20

Joe is literally mimicking each and every move Jim makes.
Sweat dripping off him.

> JOE
> (shouting)
> C'mon Jimmy, let's put on a show.
> Let's open him up for the folks.

21   INT. THE RING   21

Jim is barely holding his own. He can't get a break.
Everywhere he throws, Feldman isn't. Everywhere Feldman
throws, Jim is.

Jim is pretty lead footed, Feldman dancing all around him.
Feldman lays a combination on Jim that sends him hard into
the ropes. Folks in the audience are starting to BOO.

22   INT. THE CORNER/RING   22

Joe bobs and weaves in place.

> JOE
> You got to be first, Jimmy. Don't
> let him get set.

Jim makes a lunge, throws a wild punch, hits Feldman hard.
Jim moves in to hit him again but Feldman lowers his head.
CLOSE on Jim's fist as it connects. Bones CRACK. They clinch.

23   INT. THE CORNER - MOMENTS LATER   23

Joe is squeezing Jim's hand, his expression dark. Jim can't
hide the pain.

                         JOE
              It's broken proper, Jimmy. I'm
              calling it.

                       BRADDOCK
              I can use my left.

                         JOE
              Stay inside, don't let him crowd
              you. Do what you can with the left.

The BELL. Jim is up and into the ring. Joe shakes his head.
Looks at the Cornerman.

                         JOE
              I wish he could find his goddamn
              left.
                   (shouts)
              Shut him down!

24   INT. THE RING/CORNER - MOMENTS LATER   24

Jim is trying. But Joe's right, he just doesn't have a left
hand punch. And he's still standing in one place.

Feldman is landing punch after punch. Jim can't even use his
broken right to block. But Feldman is so hurt himself he
keeps clinching Jim in a drunken waltz. CATCALLS. SHOUTS.

IN THE CORNER

                         JOE
              Pay attention!

25   INT. THE RING   25

Jim clocks faces in the audience. SHOUTING. BOOING. Jim
throws one last right cross. He connects and the pain is a
flare, excruciating. Feldman scores a vicious right.

Jim's head SNAPS back. He manages to get Feldman in a clinch
and not let go. The BELL is hardly audible over the BOOING.

                          JOHNSTON (OVER)
                     An embarrassment.

26   INT. COMMISSION ROOM - NIGHT   26

        Smoky. Jimmy Johnston, the promoter from that first fight,
        the Ref, and the other two MEN who make up the Boxing
        Commission sit facing Joe, now standing before this makeshift
        tribunal.

                          JOHNSTON
                     That's what it was. An
                     embarrassment.

                          JOE
                     Where's the purse?

                          JOHNSTON (CONT'D)
                     I wouldn't have to tell you that if
                     you gave a shit about your fighter.

                          JOE
                     Okay, so he's fighting hurt. Maybe
                     you got fighters who can afford to
                     rest a month between fights.

                          JOHNSTON
                     Christ, he hardly gets a punch in
                     anymore. Fights getting stopped by
                     referees.... He's pathetic.

27   INT. ARMORY- HALLWAY - WALKING   27

        Joe walks the hall back to the locker room as (OVER) the
        CONVERSATION continues.

                          JOHNSTON (OVER)
                     He's was no draw tonight. And you
                     watch. Next week the gate will be
                     down by half. A fight like that
                     keeps people away.

        Joe stands at the door to the locker room.

                          JOHNSTON (OVER)
                     We're revoking his license, Joe.
                     Whatever Braddock was gonna do in
                     boxing. I guess he's done it.

28   EXT. MOUNT VERNON ARMORY - PARKING LOT - NIGHT 28

        The Men from the boxing commission move towards their cars,
        the last few vehicles left in the now abandoned parking lot.

That's when the arena door BANGS open and Jim comes out,
moving fast, Joe trailing after him.

                    BRADDOCK
          Mr. Johnston.

                    JOHNSTON
          Jim.

                    BRADDOCK
          What's going on?

                    JOHNSTON
               (to Joe)
          You didn't tell him?

                    JOE
          Yeah. I told him. But he wanted to
          hear it from you.

Johnston turns to Braddock whose right hand hangs by his
side. A look from Johnston says it all.

                    BRADDOCK
          I broke my hand, okay? You don't
          see me crying about it. I don't
          know what you got to complain
          about. We did that boondock circuit
          for you. I didn't quit on you.

Braddock's eyes are deadly.

                    BRADDOCK
          I didn't always lose. And I won't
          always lose again.

Johnston says nothing.

                    BRADDOCK
          I can still fight.

                    JOHNSTON
          Go home.

                    BRADDOCK
          I can still fight.

                    JOHNSTON
          Go home to Mae and the kids, Jim.

Johnston climbs into his car. Jim watches him drive away.

29A   INT. MOUNT VERNON ARMORY - MOMENTS LATER   29A

The ring, the bleachers, all now empty, low house lights casting long shadows.

Joe sits beside Jim, taping a broken fence board to his hand.

> JOE
> We'll splint it with this. Until we get to the hospital.

Braddock doesn't look up. Joe's VOICE softens.

> JOE
> Maybe I shouldn't have pushed you so hard, we shouldn't have gone to California that time...

Still no answer from Jim.

> JOE
> Jimmy, listen, your legs are heavy, the body lets you know...

> BRADDOCK
> Don't.

> JOE
> We're not fighting for the championship anymore. Hell, we're not even fighting for cash. And now you don't even tell me when your hand's broken before going into a fight. I'm telling you, Jim, not them, **I'm** telling you, you're too slow. It's over.

Joe keeps wrapping the tape.

> JOE
> You'd change things, sure, who wouldn't, but sometimes you just can't, you know, end of story.

Jim still hasn't looked up.

> JOE
> You waiting to see how long I can keep quiet again?

Joe grins until Braddock looks up. See this startling sight. Jim's cheeks are streaked with tears.

                    BRADDOCK
          Get me another one, Joe.

                    JOE
          Jimmy-

                    BRADDOCK
          Got to have it. We're down to our
          last buck.

                    JOE
          What's done is done.

                    BRADDOCK
          Not always.

                    JOE
          No. Not always.

In Joe's eyes, sudden awareness that this is good-bye.

                    JOE
          But this time. I'm sorry, Jimmy.

Joe finds a breath to still his own loss.

                    JOE
          I'll get the car, give you a ride
          home.

And Jim doesn't even watch Joe as he goes. PULL BACK AND UP
OVER Braddock in this giant empty space. Alone.

32   INT. BRADDOCK APARTMENT - NIGHT - MOMENTS LATER   32

Mae stands at the door as it swings open. See her relief. But
then looks up to see his battered face.

                    MAE
          Oh dear Lord. Baby...?

                    BRADDOCK
          I haven't got the money. They
          wouldn't pay me. Called it a no
          contest. Said the fight was an
          embarrassment.

But now Mae's clocked his hand, crosses to him in a
heartbeat, touching his fresh cast.

                    MAE
          What happened?

She's trying to keep the fear under control.

                    BRADDOCK
          Mr. Johnston made a decision. They
          decommissioned me.

                    MAE
          Jimmy, what happened to your hand!?

                    BRADDOCK
          It's broke in three places.

                    MAE
          Mercy. I'm so sorry.

Odd response.

                    BRADDOCK
          Said I'm through is what they said.
          Said I'm not a boxer anymore.

And now she's begun walking back and forth across the room.
Like a caged animal.

                    MAE
          Well, okay, if you can't work, we
          ain't gonna be able to pay the
          electric or the heat and we're out
          of credit at the grocery so we need
          to pack the kids, they can stay at
          my sister's temporary, I'll take in
          more sewing -

                    BRADDOCK
          Mae-

Her eyes are too wide, not quite focused.

                    MAE
          Then that way we can make two or
          three breadlines a day and then-

                    BRADDOCK
          I'll get doubles, triple shifts
          where I can find them. I'll get
          work wherever I can.

                    MAE
          Jim, you can't work. Your hand's
          broken.

                    BRADDOCK
          Mae! I can still work.

His VOICE stills her.

> BRADDOCK
> Get the shoe polish out of the
> cabinet. Go on. If they see me
> lugging this around, they won't
> pick me will they?

Finally, Mae obliges as Jim sits, extends his cast.

> BRADDOCK
> So, we'll cover it up. With the
> shoe polish.

She stares at his cast.

> BRADDOCK
> Baby, it's going to be okay.

He reaches down, lifts her chin so his eyes meet her's, both
finding tether there.

> BRADDOCK
> We still haven't seen anything we
> can't face down.

Nothing in the world now except their eyes, holding fast. And
so, finally, Mae begins blackening the cast with polish.

> MAE
> I'll cut the hem out of your coat
> sleeve, fabric will help cover it.

He kisses her head. She nearly finds a laugh.

> MAE
> All we need now is a nice piece of
> steak for your face, Jim Braddock,
> fix you right up.

Jim can't help but smile back at this woman, his wife.

> BRADDOCK
> That's a good idea. Steak. Get me a
> steak out of the ice box.
> Porterhouse.

PUSH THROUGH THE HANGING BLANKET.

Howard and Jay lay asleep in the bed in the b.g., Rosemarie
peeking around the blanket, eyes wide, watching her parents.

35   EXT. DOCKS - EARLY MORNING   35

Jim stands amidst the familiar group of MEN crowding the
gates as Jake COUNTS out the lucky ones.

Jim keeps his cast low, behind his back as NUMBERS TICK OFF.

ON JIM as his chances get less and less likely, his eyes
growing desperate, nearly willing himself to be seen.

Then, Jim is chosen. He lowers his head in relief.

36   EXT. DOCKS - MOMENTS LATER   36

Men work in pairs. Mountains of freshly unloaded flour sacks
have to be moved from loading nets to shipping palettes.

JIM'S LEFT HAND-CLOSE. Working a bailing hook into a bag,
hard, awkward work. TILT UP as Jim glances nervously at Jake.

Across from Jim, his partner, working his own hook, scowls at
the bruises on Jim's face. Handsome. Wiry. MIKE WILSON.

                    MIKE
          What the hell happened to you?

Jim glances up at him, both still working as they speak.

                    BRADDOCK
          I got into a fight.

                    MIKE
          What would you go and do that for?

                    BRADDOCK
          Good question.

                    MIKE
          Mike Wilson.

                    BRADDOCK
          Jim Braddock.

                    MIKE
          Used to follow a fighter with that
          name on the Radio.

Jim just nods.

                         MIKE
             There's another guy going around
             using that name, now, can't fight
             for shit. A gambling man could lose
             a lot of money on him. Twice.

Mike's impish smile is so winning it's contagious. That's
when a bag slips and Mike spots Jim's painted cast.

                         MIKE
             Jesus. This ain't gonna work.
             You're a cripple. You can't slow me
             down. I need this job.

                         BRADDOCK
             Look, I can hold up my end.

Mike is still working and Jim works all the harder, managing
to keep up with the other man despite his injury.

                         JAKE (OVER)
             What the hell is this?

Jake stands behind him. Staring at his casted hand. Jim looks
up at Mike and just digs his hook into his side of the bag.

It's a meaningless gesture. Unless Mike does the same. A
beat. Then Mike hooks his side and together they lift.

                         MIKE
             You see us falling behind, Jake?
             He's all right.

And they keep hooking, bag after bag, Jake watching on.
Finally Jake just shakes his head and goes.

                         BRADDOCK
             Appreciate it.

37   EXT. NEWARK - MID-DAY   37

The rain has just stopped. Women in rain coats ladle soup and
hand out soaked bread from the open back of a truck.

TRACK down the line, past so many faces, some sad. Some
embarrassed, most just emptied out by this endless loss.

FIND Mae holding a soaking Rosemarie in exhausted arms. Jay
and Howard race around their mother, shooting finger guns.

                         MAE
             Boys, settle down please.

But they have found a pair of puddles and begun a splash war.

                    MAE
          Howard! Jay!

The splashes have escalated and Howard dodges Jay's volley,
the MAN IN LINE behind him getting a good soaking.

                    MAN IN LINE
          Lady, watch your kids!

                    MAE
          Boys, come here now!
               (to the Man)
          I'm so sorry.
               (to Rosy)
          You need to stand for a little
          while, honey.

Mae starts to set her down.

                    ROSEMARIE
          I don't want to. It's wet.

Looks into her eyes.

                    MAE
          Are you a big girl or a little
          girl?

                    ROSEMARIE
               (beginning to yowl)
          Little.

Not the answer she wanted.

                    MAE
          Rosy-

                    VOICE (OVER)
          Who's making all that racket?
          Sounds like a trombone.

Jim has appeared beside them, makes a trombone of cast and
hand, and accompanying SOUND.

                    ROSEMARIE
          What's a turmone?

                    BRADDOCK
          Trom**bone,** honey. It's a musical
          instrument.

Mae is surprised but glad to see him.

                    BRADDOCK
          I got a shift. Foreman says
          tomorrow maybe a double.

Jim has moved something under his coat to his casted hand as
he takes Rosy into his arms. His boxing shoes.

                    MAE
          Are you training today?

                    BRADDOCK
          I was thinking of selling them.

The moment hangs there.

                    MAE
          Oh.

                    BRADDOCK
          I figure the three shifts and what
          I get for these, by the end of the
          week we can pay off the grocer.

                    MAE
          The Culps went on relief today.

                    BRADDOCK
          You do that there's no coming back.
          It's a downward spiral.

So much emotion in her eyes. But what she says is...

                    MAE
          Don't take less than a dollar, Jim.

He's managing a smile. Everything but his eyes.

                    BRADDOCK
          You go on home now. I'll stand.

                    MAE
          I got to turn on the heat, Jimmy.
          They're chilled through.

That's when Howard launches another SPLASH at Jay. Jim spins
and grabs his son, lifts him in the air.

                    BRADDOCK
          You know what happens to little
          monkeys who don't listen to their
          mother?

Jay is already shrieking with LAUGHTER.

                    BRADDOCK
          They get...the boot.

And Jim shoves one of his shoes into Howard's face, the
little boy promptly fake dying. Jim sets him down.

                    BRADDOCK
          Go on, now.

Mae hands him the soup pot, tows her charges along, Jim
watching them go. He turns forward again, collar going up.

HIGH AND WIDE over the crowd, all inching forward, slowly,
endlessly patient, impossible in number.

37A   INT. JEANNETTE'S GYM - DAY   37A

Joe steps out of the bathroom into the corridor, heads back
to the main floor of the gym. He freezes in the doorway.

See what he sees. Braddock stands with his old trainer Joe
Jeanette and a wiry black boxer (GEORGE), expressions somber.

                    BRADDOCK
          Joe was saying that you might need
          some shoes. I won ten fights in
          'em. Good three dollar shoes.

                    JEANNETTE
          Match them to your foot. I bet
          they fit you. Good shoes, boy.
          There you go.

                    BRADDOCK
          Gimme a New York dollar for them.

                    JEANNETTE
          Pay the man.

                    GEORGE
          I don't got a dollar though.

                    JEANNETTE
          Pay him what you got.

                    GEORGE
          I got two bits.

                    BRADDOCK
          Do me a favor. Win me a
          championship.

Jim is just handing over his shoes, for which George is giving him two bits. What few words are said, Joe can't hear.

Jim leans down, picking up his soup pot and bread to go. Jeannette spots Joe across the room. But Joe just leans back, behind the door, out of sight, as if he were never there.

> BRADDOCK (OVER)
> So first of all let me assert my firm belief that the only thing we have to fear is fear itself.

38A   INT. BRADDOCK HOME - 4:30 AM   38A

Jim sits at the table, READING Roosevelt's speech to Mae from the newspaper, trying hard to find inspiration in the words.

> BRADDOCK (OVER)
> Nameless, unreasoning, unjustified terror which paralyzes needed efforts to convert retreat into advance.

39   INT. DOCK WAREHOUSE - AFTERNOON   39

Jim and Mike daisy chain barrels. Jim using that left arm.

> BRADDOCK (OVER)
> Values have shrunken to fantastic levels: taxes have risen, our ability to pay has fallen, government of all kinds is faced by serious curtailment of income,

41   EXT. DOCKS - AFTERNOON   41

Jim is finishing his shift, dirty, just clearing the gates when PENNY runs up.

> PENNY
> They're hiring extra at the foundry.

Jim takes off in a sprint, Penny not far behind.

> BRADDOCK (OVER)
> The means of exchange are frozen in the currents of trade, the withered leaves of industrial enterprise lie on every side, farmers find no market for their produce, the savings of many years in thousands of families are gone.
>   (MORE)

                    BRADDOCK (OVER) (cont'd)
          More important, a host of
          unemployed citizens face the grim
          problem of existence and an equal
          number toil with little return.

42   EXT. FOUNDRY - NIGHT   42

        Mike shovels coal with Jim who is favoring his left hand. Jim
        pauses, his casted arm aches, resumes working that shovel.

                    BRADDOCK (OVER)
          These dark days will be worth all
          they cost us if they teach us that
          our true destiny is not to be
          ministered unto but to minister to
          ourselves and our fellow men.

43   INT. BASEMENT APARTMENT - VERY LATE   43

        Jim, black with coal dust, ENTERS, Mae dozing in a chair. He
        takes two quarters from his pocket, puts them in the jar.

        Jim stumbles towards the bed, looks at his filthy self, lays
        on the floor, instantly asleep.

                    MAE
          Jimmy, we can wash the sheets.

        But he's out cold. Mae looks at Jim a beat. Then she pulls
        the cover off their bed and lays on the floor beside him.

                    BRADDOCK (OVER)
          In the field of world policy I
          would dedicate this nation to the
          policy of the good neighbor...the
          neighbor who resolutely respects
          himself and, because he does so,
          respects the rights of others...the
          neighbor who respects his
          obligations and respects the
          sanctity of his agreements in and
          with a world of neighbors.

43A   EXT. STREET-MORNING   43A

        Jim walking towards us.

                    BRADDOCK (OVER)
          We do not distrust the future of
          essential democracy. The people of
          the United States have not failed.
          In their need they have registered
          a mandate that they want direct,
          vigorous action.
                    (MORE)

                          BRADDOCK (OVER) (cont'd)
          In this dedication of a nation, we
          humbly ask the blessing of God. May
          he protect each and every one of
          us.

Jim continues towards us, UNDER CAMERA, and gone.

46   EXT. BRADDOCK'S STREET - DAY   46

Winter has come. The world is dusted with snow. Mae has
dropped the boys at school, is walking home with Rosemarie.

                          ROSEMARIE
          Why can't I go to school yet? Is it
          because I'm a girl?

                          MAE
          Maybe. I hadn't thought of that.

A CAR drives by and from within issue the muted tones of
SINGING IN THE RAIN. Mae stares after it a beat.

                          ROSEMARIE
          Who's the man at our house?

Mae looks up to see a MAN in a PSE&G uniform standing just
outside the front door at their electric meter.

                          MAE
          Can I help you, sir?

The MAN looks at her. Sad, tired eyes.

                          PSE&G MAN
          I'm sorry, Ma'am. You're past due.

Let's the meaning sink in.

                          MAE
          You can't. There's kids. Please.

                          PSE&G MAN
          I don't, they'll let me go. They
          let two guys go for it already.

Mae stares at him.

                          MAE
          This apartment, it's what we got
          left that keeps us hanging on.

                          PSE&G MAN
          Lady. Lady, I got kids too.

The two just stand there staring at each other in the snow.

47   EXT. DOCKS - AFTERNOON   47

A FOGHORN through the falling snow signals shift's end. Jim
and Mike head away from the ships in the b.g.

47A   EXT. STREETS - WALKING   47A

Jim and Mike, exhausted, are walking down the snowy streets
when desperate SHOUTING gets their attention.

                    VOICE (V.O.)
          We got until tomorrow.

Across the street, a pleading YOUNG MAN and YOUNG WOMAN are
being evicted from a brownstone by two CITY MARSHALS.

                    YOUNG MAN
          The notice said we got another day.

Mike stares across the street, eyes darkening with rage.

                    MIKE
          Sons-a-bitches. Sons-a-goddamn-
          bitches.

Mike is gone, heading across the street. Jim frowns, follows.

                    YOUNG WOMAN (OVER)
          You can't. Once we're out we'll
          never get back in. We'll never get
          back on our feet, you see.

47B   EXT.-BROWNSTONE - CONTINUOUS   47B

The last of the furniture is being set on the sidewalk.
Surreal. Small couch. Lamp. Dresser spilling clothes.

                    YOUNG MAN
          Please, I been on relief.

The Young Woman watches as a police padlock is SNAPPED onto
the front door. The small SOUND she makes, a breaking heart.

                    YOUNG WOMAN
          We had to use the money for food.
          That's gone. But we'll have some
          for the landlord next week. Please.

                    MIKE
          Excuse me.

He stands at the curb. Nobody pays him much attention.

                    MIKE
          Excuse me!

Loud. That worked. Everybody turns.

                    MIKE
          City Marshals, right? How you boys
          doing?

The edge of pure contempt is near perfectly hidden. Mike
glances around. A few FOLKS are watching from nearby stoops.
Several more hang out windows.

                    MIKE
          You know what eviction notices are?
          Public record. **Tabulae communium.**
          They're dated, see?

He's looking around, playing the group.

                    MIKE
          But City Marshals, they've been
          known to try and get through a
          week's worth of evictions on a
          Monday, just so they don't have to
          keep coming back and forth to shit
          little towns like Weehawken.

He focuses now on the two Marshals.

                    MIKE
          You know, I bet the good people
          here would love to take a look at
          that paperwork.

He looks around. Not a MURMUR of support of support from
anyone. Somehow, that lack of support agitates him more.

                    YOUNGER MARSHAL
          Or else what?

                    MIKE
          You that kind of guy?

Mike's smile has turned lethal.

                    MIKE
          You get yourself a badge, you can
          do anything? Any time you want.

This is going nowhere good. Fast.

                    MIKE
          Push folks around. Can't do
          anything back to you-

Mike's almost moving forward when a hand stills his shoulder.
WIDER. Jim stands behind him.

                    BRADDOCK
          My friend, here. He's got lightning
          in his toes, you know. He don't
          mean nothing by it.

The moment lasts.

                    YOUNGER MARSHAL
          Jim Braddock, ain't it?

                    OLDER MARSHAL
          Yeah. I thought it was you.

Impossible not to feel his physical presence.

Then the older cop looks down at his paper.

                    OLDER MARSHAL
          Maybe we got our days mixed up.

Mike nods. Forces a smile.

                    OLDER MARSHAL
          Seen you fight, Jim.

                    MIKE
          So, you boys want to help us move
          their furniture back in?

                    YOUNGER MARSHAL
          Don't push your luck, fella.

The young couple are staring in awe at the departing cops.
But Mike has already grabbed the dresser, gestures to Jim. A
few neighbors join, all helping the couple move back in.

48   INT.- QUINCY'S BAR - AFTERNOON   48

Smoky. Sawdust on plank floors. MEN from the docks. Jim and
Mike stand at the bar as QUINCY comes to take their order.

                    MIKE
          I'll get a cold beer.

                    BRADDOCK
          Water for me please, Quincy.

                         QUINCY
          All I got today, big spenders.

In fact, many of the men there are drinking only water. But
apparently, Mike's having none of it.

                         MIKE
          Beer for him too. I'm buying.

Jim starts to protest. Mike just raises his hand.

                         MIKE
          Don't hurt my feelings.

Mike pays for the beers and they move to a table.

                         BRADDOCK
          So you a lawyer?

                         MIKE
          Stock Broker. But I hired so many
          of the bastards, might as well a
          been to law school myself. Still
          lost it all.

A simple number says it all.

                         MIKE
          '29.

Jim nods, takes a sip. Liquid gold.

                         BRADDOCK
          Me too. Had just about everything I
          ever earned in stocks. Even had a
          little taxi company. I mean who
          loses money on cabs in New York
          City?

Jim smiles, opens his hand, as if to say, all gone. The two
sit there, a moment of silent understanding.

                         MIKE
          You know they got people living in
          Central Park and eating the sheep.
          Calling it the Hooverville.

Mike's getting worked up.

                         MIKE
          Government's dropped us flat. We
          need to organize. Unionize. Fight
          back.

                    BRADDOCK
          Whoa. Fight what? Bad luck? Greed?
          Drought? No use boxing what you
          can't see, friend.

Jim throws an easy smile.

                    BRADDOCK
          I like what FDR says, you gotta
          trust in essential democracy-

                    MIKE
          Screw FDR. FDR. Hoover. They're all
          the same. I come home one day and
          stand in my living room and
          somewhere between the mortgage and
          the market and the goddamn lawyer
          who was supposed to be working for
          me it stopped being mine. It all
          stopped being mine. FDR hasn't
          given me my house back yet.

Mike's getting worked up.

                    MIKE
          Russia, right now, they're giving
          the factories back to the workers.

                    BRADDOCK
          In Russia, right now, I'm pretty
          sure they're asleep, Mike.

Mike lifts his beer.

                    MIKE
          Even this. You know why they
          repealed prohibition? You think its
          about freedom? It's about federal
          revenue collection, plain simple.

Mike drains his glass.

                    MIKE
          How about another one, Jim?

Jim's tempted. Then, rising...

                    BRADDOCK
          Thanks, Mike. But I gotta go home.

                    MIKE
          Hey, Braddock. I know I talk too
          much. But it wasn't just me.

Mike is looking up at him.

                    MIKE
          You did some good out there. You
          have a good night.

Jim might respond. But Mike's already heading for the bar.

48A   EXT. BRADDOCK APARTMENT - NIGHT   48A

Hard snow piles against the building in growing drifts.

49   INT. BRADDOCK APARTMENT - NIGHT   49

The blanket that usually divides the apartment is piled, with
all remaining coats and clothing, over the kids in bed. Jim
stands over them, watching their breath fog as they sleep.

                    MAE
          You think about it, you gotta go to
          a swanky joint to eat with candles.

Mae finishes lighting candles as Jim crosses to throw wood
from a pile of broken sign scraps into the oven fire.

Mae sits, empties the mason jar onto the table as Jim joins
her, adds the few meager coins from his pocket.

                    BRADDOCK
          Six bucks seventy. How much to turn
          it back on?

                    MAE
          Three months. Thirty-three ten.

Jim moves the money around on the table. Nowhere near.

                    BRADDOCK
          If I work 26 hours out of every 24,
          it still won't add up. And we got
          nothing left to sell.

Jim's trying to stay calm.

                    BRADDOCK
          All my busted bones, then a piece
          of paper changes hands and that's
          it. It's all for nothing.

Mae takes Jim's hands in hers. He smiles up at his wife.

                    BRADDOCK
          All the guys you could have
          married.

                    MAE
          Yeah. What happened to those guys?

She smiles at him.

                    MAE
          I married the man I love.

(OVER) A child's WET COUGH. Jim glances up at her sharply.

                    MAE
          Howard. Since this afternoon.

Mae folds her hands before her. She closes her eyes, begins
to pray. Then glances up at her husband.

                    MAE
          Jim...?

                    BRADDOCK
          I'm all prayed out.

It only takes a look from Mae for Jim to start back-peddling.

                    BRADDOCK
          God's too busy for me right now. He
          already gave me you and the kids.
          He's answered all my prayers.

Jim's up and moving across the room. She can't see the
darkness in his eyes.

                    BRADDOCK
          He doesn't owe me anything.

50   INT. BRADDOCK APARTMENT - FIRST LIGHT   50

The light before dawn. Mae sleeps with the kids under the
pile of clothes. Still freezing. She stirs. Jim is gone.

51   EXT. STREET - MORNING   51

Mae and the children stand at the base of a giant framed
billboard showing a smiling man and his Gillette razor.

Mae looks around. Streets empty save for two more children,
dirtier than hers, doing laundry in the runoff at the curb.

Mae begins breaking off pieces of wooden latticework from the
billboard frame, hands the scraps to her still sleepy kids.

                    WOMAN'S VOICE (OVER)
          Where are you going?

Mae looks up. A WOMAN hangs out a brownstone window,
SHOUTING, rage so great she seems not to know she is crying.

                    WOMAN
          Go ahead you piece of shit.

The MAN walking away down the block is holding a small, twine
tied suitcase. He doesn't even turn, back bowed by shame.

                    WOMAN
          Go on then. We don't need you.

One of the children in the gutter, a small BOY, stares after
the Man. Then he turns and locks sad eyes with Mae.

                    MAE
              (finally pulling away)
          Come on, now, let's go.

She sweeps her children in front of her, towards home.

52   INT. BRADDOCK APARTMENT - DAY   52

Snow cakes the windows. Mae is feeding the stove with lattice
chips. Howard, fever worse, sits under covers by the fire.

                    MAE
          Baby, look at Mommy.

Mae kneels, rubs him, fever making him shake in the cold.
Mae tucks in the blankets, forces a water glass to his lips.

                    MAE
          Drink up, now.

Howard manages a couple of sips. Mae tucks the covers around
him, unaware of the sudden tears spilling from her eyes.

                    JAY
          Mommy?

She looks down at her son, his fear at seeing her sadness.

                    MAE
          It's all right sweetheart. Mommy'll
          be right back.

Mae rises, EXITS the back door.

53   EXT. BRADDOCK APARTMENT - BACK YARD - CONTINUOUS   53

A tiny square of dirt amidst the buildings. Heavy snow is
falling. Mae stands alone, BREATHLESS WEEPING, inconsolable.

54   INT. BRADDOCK APARTMENT - AFTERNOON   54

Jim ENTERS. The last cinders of Mae's sidewalk fire glow. The
room is dark. Cold.

Mae sits in her coat, face empty, hollowed out. She looks up
at Jim as he stares at her in the empty apartment.

                    MAE
          Howard's fever was getting worse.
          And then Rosy started to sneeze.

Jim looks around. No sign of the children.

                    BRADDOCK
          Where are they, Mae?

She looks up at him, finally.

                    MAE
          We can't even keep them warm.

                    BRADDOCK
          Where are they Mae?

See the agony in her eyes.

                    MAE
          The boys'll sleep on the sofa at my
          father's in Brooklyn. Rosy's going
          to stay at my sister's. We can't
          keep them, Jim.

He stares at her, his emotions impossible to express.

                    BRADDOCK
          You don't decide what happens to
          our children without me.

                    MAE
          Jimmy, if they get real sick, we
          don't have the money for a doctor.

                    BRADDOCK
          You send them away, this has all
          been for nothing.

There is a cold anger in his eyes. But something else that
more resembles heartbreak

> MAE
> It's only until we can make enough
> to get back to even, then we can-

> BRADDOCK
> If it was that easy, why didn't I
> just go on relief, get a book and
> put my feet up. Every day, out
> there, it was so we could stay
> together. What else was it for? If
> we can't stay together, it means we
> lost.

> MAE
> Baby, no one has any good choices
> anymore, we'll get them-

> BRADDOCK
> Mae. I promised him, see? I got on
> my knees, looked in his eyes and I
> promised him I would never send him
> away.

Jim is heading for the door.

> MAE
> What are you doing?

54A   EXT. BRADDOCK APARTMENT   54A

As Jim heads down the block, Mae SHOUTS after him.

> MAE
> Where are you going? Jimmy, come
> back!

She covers her mouth, staring after her husband.

54B   INT. NEWARK RELIEF OFFICE - DAY   54B

At a counter at the front of a long line a stern faced WOMAN
counts out twelve dollars eighty for a shame-ridden Jim.

> WOMAN
> I would never have expected to see
> you here, Jim.

56   EXT. FERRY - DAY   56

Jim, on the deck, looks towards the Manhattan skyline.

57   EXT. EIGHTH AVENUE - DAY   57

Jim walks past boarded up store fronts. A young GIRL (12)
stands in a doorway, sad eyes and outfit of inappropriate
promise.

58   EXT. LEXINGTON AVENUE   58

Jim continues his endless walk. A MAN in a suit sells apples,
none very appealing.

Jim passes a department store as a limo pulls curb-side and
two well-to-do children race out followed by their parents.

Jim walks through a milling crowd in front of an employment
office without even pausing.

59   EXT. MADISON SQUARE GARDEN - DAY   59

Men are tearing down the light board for scrap. Jim stares at
mounted photos of boxers in fight stances. Heads inside.

60   INT. MADISON SQUARE GARDEN - BOXING CLUB - DAY   60

Thick with smoke. Maybe twenty MEN sit around, playing cards.
Loud ARGUMENTS. Johnston. Gould.

TWO PROMOTERS stand LAUGHING. They don't even notice Jim
ENTER. Not until he's standing right in front of them.

                    BRADDOCK
          Mr. Allen. Phil.

This is almost killing him.

                    BRADDOCK
          Thing is. I can't afford to pay the
          heat. Had to farm out my kids.

Every word is impossible.

                    BRADDOCK
          They keep cutting shifts at the
          dock. You don't get picked every
          day. Just need enough to catch up.

The shame almost too much to bear.

                    BRADDOCK
          Went to the relief office. Gave me
          twelve eighty. I need thirteen
          sixty more. To pay the bill. Get
          them back.

This once great fighter now takes off his hat.

> BRADDOCK
> It pains me to ask. So much. But I
> sure would be grateful.

He holds out his hat. The moment lasts. The room has grown silent. The two men are speechless. Then one digs into his pocket, comes out with a few coins.

> PROMOTER
> Sure, Jim. Sure.

> BRADDOCK
> Thank you.

The next guy does the same. What follows is nearly too excruciating to watch. Jim moves around the room, hat in hand. Even Johnston gives. The last man he comes on is Joe. Jim can barely meet his eyes.

> BRADDOCK
> I'm sorry, Joe.

> JOE
> What the hell do you have to be
> sorry about? Jesus, Jim.

Jim is looking into the hat.

> JOE
> How short are you?

Jim's been counting as he goes.

> BRADDOCK
> A buck-fifty, I think.

Joe winces, goes into his wallet. Fishes out a single, two quarters. Puts them in the hat.

> BRADDOCK
> Joe...

> JOE
> Don't mention it, Jimmy.

They watch him go, one of their own, nothing left, not even his pride. HOLD on JOE GOULD.

61   INT. BRADDOCK HOUSE - NIGHT   61

Mae flicks on the lights. They work. The children spill into
the glowing apartment.

HOLD on Jim as he stands in the doorway, spent, acutely aware
of how fragile home is.

62   EXT. CHURCH YARD - SPRING - 1934 - DAY   62

Mike, Penny and several others from the docks sit on benches
at the edge of the church yard, away from the gathering of
families on the common. They pass a bottle back and forth.

                    PENNY
          Half shifts don't do nobody no
          good.

Jim approaches from the street in work clothes.

                    MIKE
          What we need, boys, is a union. In
          Russia, right now, they're giving
          the factories to the workers.

                    BRADDOCK
          In Russia, right now, I'm pretty
          sure they're asleep.

Jim has arrived, stops to join them. Mike smiles, gestures to
with the bottle. Braddock's tempted but just shakes his head.

                    PENNY
          You need to shut up with that
          Bolshivist crap or Jake's gonna cut
          you and the rest of us too.

Jim looks across the yard to see two WOMEN emerge from the
church basement. Each holds a frosted sheet cake.

                    MIKE
          Long live The Revolution!

Jim glances at the bottle in Mike's hand.

                    BRADDOCK
          Long live Johnny Walker too.

Mike's words are for only Jim.

                    MIKE
          Can't be afraid all the time.

Jim nods, heads on towards the common, Mike watching him go.

63   EXT. CHURCH YARD - SPRING - 1934   63

A gathering of families in the church yard. Jim stands, his
cast gone, with Mae, the kids and FATHER RORICK as two
frosted sheet cakes are set on the picnic table, burning
candles like tiny stars.

                  CROWD
        Happy birthday to you. Happy
        birthday to you. Happy birthday
        dear...

A SERIES OF SHOTS - MEN AND WOMEN - SAME MOMENT

                  WOMAN
        Mitchell.

                  MAN
        Junior.

                  GIRL
        Philip.

                  OLD MAN
        Lisa.

                  MAE
        Jay.

BACK TO SCENE

The crowd finishes.

                  CROWD
        Happy birthday to you.

                  HOWARD
        I liked it more when we had our
        own.

                  FATHER RORICK
        Your Dad ever tell you I used to
        spar with him?

                  HOWARD
        You hit the Father?

                  BRADDOCK
        As often as possible.

Jim shares Rorick's smile as the kids take off. Rorick
glances at his church behind him.

>   FATHER RORICK
>   We miss you in service, Jim.

>   BRADDOCK
>   I get an extra shift.

Rorick's nod knows there's more to it than that.

>   BRADDOCK
>   You ever ask yourself, what's the
>   reason?

>   FATHER RORICK
>   He has his reasons. We are His
>   children, Jim.

>   BRADDOCK
>   I'm sure He does, Tom, but how'd
>   you feel about me if I treated my
>   kids like this?

Rorick is about to respond when Mae's VOICE cuts him off.

>   MAE
>   (terse)
>   James.

Jim follows her darkening gaze.

64   EXT. CHURCH YARD - BENCH AREA - MOMENTS LATER   64

Mike is off to the side of the common at a picnic table,
facing his WIFE (SARA, 30's) and INFANT DAUGHTER. A couple of
folks have already turned towards the COMMOTION.

>   SARA
>   Everyday, fix the world. How about
>   fixing your family? What kind of
>   father are you? Too proud to cross
>   the lawn because she can't have her
>   own birthday cake. And now you're
>   drunk at church for Christ's sake.

>   MIKE
>   That a joke, Sara? Are you making a
>   joke?

>   SARA
>   I'm just saying it's enough!

Jim walks up to the two of them.

> BRADDOCK
> Hey, where's the ref?

> MIKE
> This is between husband and wife,
> Jim.

> SARA
> How do you even call yourself that?

Mike actually moves towards her. Not clear what he's going to do, if anything. Jim stops him with a firm hand to chest.

> BRADDOCK
> (smiling)
> Easy there, Mike. Maybe you've had
> a couple. No harm in that. Day of
> rest after all.

But Mike isn't smiling back. He's staring into Jim's eyes.

> MIKE
> That the way it is? Man'll take
> your beer long as you're paying...

Mike shoves Braddock. Like trying to push a truck.

> BRADDOCK
> There's no need for you to do this.

> MIKE
> Jim Braddock, big fighter...

Mike throws a punch which Jim slaps away easily.

> BRADDOCK
> Mike, I got no beef with you.

> MIKE
> Couldn't make it in the ring...

Throws another, which Jim's hand also dismisses, Mike SHOUTING now.

> MIKE
> Why not take it out on his pal-

Mike goes to grab Jim and Jim shoves him aside, but Mike trips, hits his head on the cement path, spilling blood.

                    SARA
          Jim, no-.

She's moved to Mike who is scrambling up. Stares at Jim.

                    MIKE
          Go to hell. Both of you.

And with that Mike is gone. Sara stares at him. Then she
turns to Jim, the baby WAILING in her arms.

                    SARA
          Jesus, Jim, He wasn't going to hit
          me. Jesus.

And with that she's gone after her husband. Jim looks up to
see Mae standing a few feet off.

                    MAE
          Why was it so hard just to come
          over for the cake?

Too much adrenaline everywhere.

                    BRADDOCK
               (flaring)
          Maybe he just needed a little time,
          all right. It's not so damned easy.
          Maybe he just needed a little time.

                    MAE
               (flaring back)
          Not at me, James Braddock. Do you
          hear? I know its hard. But not. At.
          Me.

The two stand facing each other. Feet and miles away.

65   EXT. STREET - SUNDAY - DAY   65

Spring can still be beautiful. Even here and now. Jay and
Howard play stick ball with other kids in the street.

Jim arrives to find Rosemarie watching from a stoop. He sits
with her as Jay appears, grabbing a stray ball.

                    JAY
          No second shifts at the yards, dad?

                    BRADDOCK
          Yeah, but they only want kids. Go
          grab a shovel.

But as Jay grins and takes off, we can see Jim's worry.

>   ROSEMARIE
>   Were you and that man fighting?

Jim turns to her. Standing on the step above the one on which
he sits, they are the same height.

>   BRADDOCK
>   We were **almost** fighting.

>   ROSEMARIE
>   Teach me how.

>   BRADDOCK
>   I can't, honey.

>   ROSEMARIE
>   Why not?

>   BRADDOCK
>   Because the cops might come back.

>   ROSEMARIE
>   You mean, Mommy?

Jim nods somberly. Rosy puts her hands on her hips.

>   ROSEMARIE
>   You can too. Teach me daddy.

Jim tries to stare down his daughter. He's just no match.

>   BRADDOCK
>   Look, it's about balance. Put your
>   right here, twist your hips and
>   throw that one...

Rosemarie obliges. Awfully serious. Awfully cute.

>   BRADDOCK
>   Wow. Look at that. You got a better
>   jab than I did.

That's when a familiar car pulls up, window rolling down.

>   JOE
>   You **are** a brave man.

>   BRADDOCK
>   Not really. Mae's at the store.

Rosemarie, taking advantage of the distraction, clocks Jim sqaure in the jaw. Not bad for someone pint-sized.

>   BRADDOCK
>   (laughing)
>   Okay, darling. Good shot. Shadow
>   punch while I talk to uncle Joe.

Rosemarie punches the air as Jim rises, walks to Joe who has emerged from the car. Jim touches the lapel of his suit.

>   BRADDOCK
>   Still looking dapper, I see.

>   JOE
>   Gotta keep up appearances.

Joe smiles.

>   JOE
>   Good to see you, Jimmy.

Jim smiles back. Neither may have known it until now but these two missed each other. Joe looks around. Casual.

>   JOE
>   Nice day.

>   BRADDOCK
>   You drive all the way out here to
>   talk about the weather?

>   JOE
>   Maybe I was in the neighborhood.

>   BRADDOCK
>   Joe, this is Jersey.

>   JOE
>   A point.

A beat. Then...

>   JOE
>   I got you a fight.

>   BRADDOCK
>   Go to Hell.

>   JOE (CONT'D)
>   You want it don't you?

                    BRADDOCK
          What about the Commission?

                    JOE
          They'll sanction it. This one time
          and one time only. This isn't a
          comeback. This is one fight.

                    BRADDOCK
          Why?

                    JOE
          Because of who you're...

                    BRADDOCK
          How much?

                    JOE
          Just once ask me who you're
          fighting.

                    BRADDOCK
          How much?

                    JOE
          $250.00 You're on the big show at
          the Garden...tomorrow night.

Joe is trailing him.

                    JOE
          You fight Corn Griffin, Jimmy.
          Number 2 heavyweight contender in
          the world. Prelim before the
          championship bout.

Jim finally spins on him, intense, dangerous.

                    BRADDOCK
          Joe, this isn't funny.

                    JOE
          It ain't no favor. Griffin's
          opponent got cut and can't fight.
          They needed somebody they could
          throw in on a day's notice. Nobody
          legit will take a fight against
          Griffin without training so...

Joe looks away. Looks back at Jim.

                    JOE
          I told them they could use the
          angle Griffin was gonna knock out a
          guy'd never been knocked out
          before. You're meat, Jimmy.

                    BRADDOCK
          You on the level?

                    JOE
          Always.

Jim's still looking at his friend. Then he smiles.

                    BRADDOCK
          Joe. For 250 bucks I'd fight *your*
          wife.

                    JOE
          Now you are dreaming.

HOLD on Rosemarie as she listens to the adults TALK,
something working in her tiny mind.

65A   INT.-BRADDOCK APARTMENT -NIGHT   65A

Dark. Quiet. Jim lies asleep in his bed. PULL BACK to FIND
Mae alone in the chair, eyes red, staring at her husband.

66   INT. BUTCHER SHOP - DAY   66

(OVER) TAPPING. SAM, a butcher, emerges from the back, walks
towards his closed door. Rosemarie stands TAPPING the glass.

                    SAM
               (opening the door)
          We're closed, today.

Rosemarie walks past him to the counter. The two boys follow.

                    SAM
               (off Jay)
          Well, look who's here. Should I
          lock everything up?

Jay flushes deep red.

                    ROSEMARIE
          Let me tell him. I need a piece of
          meat, sir.

She eyes the case and the few remaining cuts of meat.

                    ROSEMARIE
          Peter's house.

                    SAM
          Porterhouse?

Rosemarie nods seriously.

                    SAM
          You got any money?

Rosemarie shakes her head no.

                    ROSEMARIE
          How about something you dropped on
          the floor?

                    SAM
          I don't drop it. And if I do I
          clean it off. Its too precious.

                    ROSEMARIE
          It's not for me.

                    SAM
          Who's it for?

Sam stares at her. Intrigued by so small a person this
intense and complete.

                    ROSEMARIE
          My Dad. He needs it so he can win a
          boxing fight.

HOLD on Sam's perplexed expression.

67   EXT. MADISON SQUARE GARDEN BOWL - LONG ISLAND CITY -NIGHT 67

The MARQUEE reads: **PRIMO CARNERA vs. MAX BAER**
                        HEAVY-WEIGHT CHAMPIONSHIP
                        TITLE FIGHT!
                        - And 6 Other Fights -

68   INT. DRESSING ROOM - CONTINUOUS   68

Jim, in his trunks, is taping up his hands. Joe ENTERS with a
robe, shoes, and gloves.

                    JOE (OVER)
          I mean, Chrissakes, a hundred and
          something fights, you never been
          knocked out, for God's sake who
          goes and sells his gear?

Joe drops the stuff in front of Jim. Shakes his head.

                    JOE (CONT'D)
          Borrowed gear, borrowed robe.

Jim lifts a shoe. It's bright red, like a clown's.

                    BRADDOCK
          Maybe I oughta get an Aooga horn,
          chase him around the ring.

                    JOE
          You been drinking?

                    BRADDOCK
          Now why go hurt my feelings?

                    JOE
          Well, you're too loose, you're
          spooking me. Sharpen up.

                    BRADDOCK
          Come on, Joe, we both know what
          this is, right?

Braddock smiles, a deep, sad smile.

                    BRADDOCK
          I get to put a little more distance
          between my kids and the street. And
          say good-bye at the Garden with a
          full house night of a big fight.

Joe has begun lacing his shoe.

                    BRADDOCK
          What's Griffin gonna show me that I
          ain't already seen?

There is a loud GROWLING NOISE.

                    JOE
          What the hell was that?

                    BRADDOCK
          They ran out of soup on the line
          this morning.

                    JOE
          How the hell you gonna fight on an
          empty stomach?

69   INT. MSG BOWL - RINGSIDE - NIGHT   69

FORD BOND, the Radio Announcer, is on the air...

                    BOND
          Good Evening! Welcome to tonight's
          broadcast of the Primo Carnera -
          Max Baer fight for the heavyweight
          championship of the world!

The Garden is filling up.

70   INT. DRESSING BOOM - NIGHT   70

Jim waits. Joe ENTERS, carrying a bowl.

                    JOE
          Hash is all they had. Eat quick.

                    BRADDOCK
          Where's the spoon?

                    JOE
          It's not there?

Joe glances at the clock on the wall.

                    JOE
          You gotta go anyway.

                    BRADDOCK
               (sniffing again)
          One bite.

Jim starts to dip his hand into the hash.

                    JOE
          Hey! I don't have time to re-tape
          you! Sit tight, I'll find one.

Joe rushes out again. Jim stares at the bowl in his hand. The
aroma nearly makes him salivate. A long beat.

Jim shoves his face into the bowl, eating like a dog.

                    VOICE (OVER)
          Good God. Am I seeing a ghost? An
          apparition?

Jim looks up, his face smeared with hash.

                    VOICE (OVER)
          Isn't that James J. Braddock, the
          Bulldog of Bergen?

A MAN with a press pass, reporter's pad and a pencil behind
his ear stands in the open door. SPORTY LEWIS.

                    SPORTY
          Saw your name on the card. Thought
          it had to be a different guy.

Jim says nothing, just stands, wipes his mouth with a towel.
Sporty throws a few shadow punches.

                    SPORTY
          Come on, Jimmy. How's that right?
          No hello for your old pal?

Braddock quotes words seared onto his memory.

                    BRADDOCK
          New York Herald. July 18, 1929.
          Byline Sporty Lewis. Proving Jim
          Braddock was too young, too green
          and rushed to the top, Loughran
          wiped the ring with the bulldog's
          career. A sad and somber funeral
          with body still breathing.

That look in Braddock's eyes just killed Sporty's smile.

                    SPORTY
          Look, Braddock, I don't fight the
          fights. I just write about them.

Braddock puts his forehead right down to Sporty's.

                    BRADDOCK
          Save that crap for the customers.

That grin of Jim's gets wider. Lethal.

                    BRADDOCK
          You got me?

The moment lasts. That's when a Garden Official appears in
the door.

                    OFFICIAL (CONT'D)
          You're on, pal.

Braddock disengages, grabs his robe, heads out. Sporty stares
after him, clearly shaken. Turns to the Official.

                              SPORTY
                    That guy. What a wash-out.

71   INT. RINGSIDE - DAY   71

Sporty Lewis climbs back ringside, amidst other reporters,
noses up against the cloth.

                         YOUNG REPORTER
                         (off his card)
                    Who's Jim Braddock?

Jim and Joe have begun making their way through the crowd in
the b.g. Few pay them much attention.

                              SPORTY
                    Get your pencil out, kid. I got
                    your lead line for you. The walk
                    from the locker room to the ring
                    was the only time tonight that old
                    Jim Braddock was seen on his feet.

Jim climbs into the ring to warm up. He is wearing a robe
with the name *Fred Carston* written on the back.

                         YOUNG REPORTER
                         (even more confused)
                    Who's Fred Carston?

72   INT. QUINCY'S BAR - CONTINUOUS   72

Packed with water drinkers. Quincy couldn't be less thrilled.
Guys from the docks sit with Mike as the RADIO warms up.

                            BOND (V.O.)
                    Well it seems Jim Braddock has come
                    out of retirement just for tonight!

All look at each other.

                            DOCK GUY
                    Can't be...

They all look at Mike, who shakes his head and opens his
hands, as shocked as everyone else.

73   INT. THE RING - CONTINUOUS   73

The crowd is WILD with CHEERS.

                          RING ANNOUNCER
                    ...Corn Griffin.

At 6'2", 210 lbs., GRIFFIN claps his gloves, powerful, confident, the "Golden Boy" of heavyweight contenders.

> RING ANNOUNCER
> And in this corner, from North
> Bergen, New Jersey...Jim Braddock.

No reaction from the crowd.

74   INT. RING - NIGHT   74

The BELL. Griffin comes out punching hard and fast. Jim is doing all he can to keep the blows from connecting. But Griffin's hands are like a storm coming from everywhere.

It only takes a second to realize this fight was a bad idea. Griffin is in perfect form. His jabs and body shots are perfect. Jim clinches. Corn straightens him with an uppercut.

75   INT. THE CORNER   75

Joe is blocking in time with Jim, his arms and body dancing in an echoing shadow play of the fight. Like the old days.

> JOE
> (shouts)
> Step inside those hooks, Jim. Keep
> your head down.

76   INT. THE RING   76

Griffin throws a right which Jim blocks with his left. Jim seems surprised by his own move.

Griffin throws a haymaker that connects to the side of Jim's head. Jim looks as if he's trying to do a cartwheel. Jim goes down, hard, onto the mat.

77   INT. QUINCY'S BAR - CONTINUOUS   77

> BOND (V.O.)
> Oh! And Braddock is down! A
> thunderous left hook from Griffin
> sends Braddock to the mat!

MURMURS all around. What else could be expected? Only Mike gestures for quiet, stares at the radio.

78   INT. THE RING   78

The Ref stands over Jim.

                              REF
                    One...Two...three...

*FLASH - Jim looks up watches himself getting hit. The moment
runs backwards and forwards, backwards and forwards.*

                              REF
                    Four...five...six...

Jim starts to rise.

78A   INT. RING - AT THE APRON - CONTINUOUS   78A

                              JOE
                    Hey. What's the rush? Two lefts,
                    Jimmy. Pop pop.

78B   INT. RING - CONTINUOUS   78B

Jim finally stands. Shaky on his feet as a new colt, blood
streaming from a cut inside his mouth.

                           REFEREE
                    It's over, Braddock.

Jim looks over the Ref's head at Griffin. Manages a smile.

                          BRADDOCK
                    He don't look that bad, Bill!

The Ref shakes his head, starts to raise his hand to stop the
fight. Jim puts his gloves on the Ref's arm.

                      BRADDOCK (CONT'D)
                    Billy. Please. Let me go.

The Ref hesitates then steps aside. Griffin practically runs
into Jim's corner. He misses Jim's head but lands a left to
the body with an ugly thud. Jim gets in two jabs with the
left before the BELL. No one seems more surprised than Jim.

78C   INT. THE CORNER - SECONDS LATER   78C

Jim sits, really beaten on.

                              JOE
                    You're doing great Jimmy. Run him
                    all over the ring. He's big, he's
                    going to get tired real fast. You
                    know the two jabs work. You gotta
                    get your right in faster. You got
                    to stop some of those left hands.

> BRADDOCK
> You don't see any of them getting
> by me do you?

78D   INT. RING - SECONDS LATER   78D

Jim moves a little better, but still can't avoid the pursuing
Griffin who is working for a knockout. Jim manages to land a
jab or two. He tries to throw his right but is clipped by a
quicker Griffin left hook, but Jim escapes being cornered.

79   INT. THE CORNER - SECONDS LATER   79

Jim's face is swelling with knots. Joe stands in front of him
and pours water, which Jim spits out, puts his head down.

> JOE
> He's a half step behind you. You're
> opening him up like a tomato can.
> If you don't believe me sway. Sway,
> see what happens. Two jabs and the
> big apple. Pop. Pop. Bang.

80   INT. THE RING - CONTINUOUS   80

The Bell CLANGS.

Jim moves out. Corn comes out jabbing. Jim is fading off of
him. After two jabs, Jim sways. He steps into Corn as Corn
throws the next punch. Jim blocks. Corn throws an upper cut
that pushes Jim into the corner. Jim sweeps underneath him,
two jabs and a mighty right to Corn. Pop, pop, bang. Corn
goes down. The Ref begins COUNTING.

81   INT. CORNER - CONTINUOUS   81

Joe was shadow punching, throwing his right. Looks down at
his own left hand. More stunned than Griffin.

> JOE
> Glory, hallelujah, where the hell
> you been, Jimmy Braddock?

82   INT. RING - CONTINUOUS   82

> REF
> ...Three.

Griffin is up. Jim charges in two steps. Begins a series of
punches, impossible in force and number.

82A   INT. - CORNER - CONTINUOUS   82A

                      JOE
                 (apoplectic)
No daylight! Close the shutters!
Bring down the curtains. Throw him
in the slammer! Send him back to
the Ozarks or wherever the hell.

82B   INT. - RING - CONTINUOUS   82B

Jim's punches keep coming, as if in the thousands, ever more
precise and now a hard right.

(OVER) The CROWD shares an intake of BREATH. Griffin just
stares at him, as if in shock. The moment lasts. Then Griffin
goes down head first, as if his skull has suddenly filled
with thoughts too heavy to hold. And he stays there.

Absolute stunned silence. Sporty Lewis is frog-eyed.

83   INT. QUINCY'S BAR - CONTINUOUS   83

                    BOND (OVER)
This is unbelievable! Corn Griffin,
the number 2 contender in the
world, has been knocked out by Jim
Braddock in the 3rd round!

Quincy's is utter MAYHEM. In the center of it all, Mike just
shakes his head and smiles.

                    MIKE
That a boy, Jimmy. That a boy.

84   INT. MADISON SQUARE GARDEN BOWL - LONG ISLAND CITY -NIGHT 84

The Ref is holding up Jim's hand in triumph. Joe jumps onto
Jim's back. The crowd is on their feet, SCREAMING.

85   INT. DRESSING ROOM - LATER   85

Jim finishes that cold hash with a spoon. Door SLAMS and
whirlwind Joe blows into the room.

                    JOE
Jesus, mother and Joseph, Mary and
all the saints and martyrs and
Jesus, ---did I say Jesus---, where
the hell did that left come from?

                  BRADDOCK
Yeah, you did. Say Jesus.

Their old easy rhythm.

> BRADDOCK
> (of the spoon)
> Good they invented these.

> JOE
> The left, Jimmy.

Jim looks at his own left.

> BRADDOCK
> When my hand was broke. On the
> docks. I had to use my left to
> work.

Opens and closes that fist.

> BRADDOCK
> Got lucky, I guess.

> JOE
> That's something you ain't been in
> a long time.

> BRADDOCK
> Everybody's due.

> JOE
> Due or not, I'll take it.

> BRADDOCK
> That was on Hash. Imagine what I
> could have done on a couple of
> steaks.

> JOE
> Wipe your mouth. You still remember
> how to satisfy the baying hounds?

Joe has already put his hand on the door, turns back. His
final words are soft, for Jim only.

> JOE
> That was one hell of a goodbye.

Joe pulls open the door to several SHOUTING reporters.

> JOE
> Here boys.

> REPORTERS
> Braddock! Jim! Braddock!

86   INT. MSG BOWL - OUTSIDE THE DRESSING ROOMS - LATER   86

Jim and Joe are heading down the corridor. They stop at the
edge of the ring, look up at the fight that's raging.

MAX BAER, the young lion of the boxing world, is 6'3", 210
beautifully proportioned pounds, handsome. He is fighting...

PRIMO CARNERA, 6'7" 270, an awesome giant and Heavyweight
Champion of the World.

                    JOE
                (off Baer)
        Imagine *that* hitting you?

                    BRADDOCK
        How about that guy we bought the
        cab company from?

                    JOE
        That's an idea.

In this theatre in the round, Baer is smashing Carnera to the
mat with his fists. Carnera, bloody and beaten, staggers to
his feet. Baer arrogantly taunts the giant.

87   INT. THE RING - CONTINUOUS   87

                    BOND (V.O.)
        Primo Carnera has been knocked down
        for what has to be a record 11
        times! And Max Baer struts around
        the ring in utter contempt of the
        Heavyweight Champion of the World!

Carnera's massive bulk is heaving with fatigue and shock. He
pushes the Ref aside and staggers toward Baer.

Baer waits, smiling, steps out from the corner and blasts
Carnera over and over again. A massacre. Jim and Joe can't
believe their eyes.

PUSH IN ON Sporty, near the ring, watching them.

88   EXT. BRADDOCK HOUSE - NIGHT   88

Jim stands facing the front door. He hasn't touched the knob
when it swings open, Jim staring down as if in defeat.

                    BRADDOCK
        I won.

The kids SHOUT in GLEE behind her. He grins. Mae just stands there, entirely unsure what to say.

89   INT. BRADDOCK HOUSE - MINUTES LATER   89

Mae is at the stove. Jim is staring in awe at the piece of raw meat that Rosemarie is holding up to him.

                    ROSEMARIE
          Put it on your eyes.

                    BRADDOCK
          Where did you get this?

Jim throws a look at Jay. Mae shakes her head.

                    MAE
          They snuck off, which we had a *long*
          talk about.
                (scowls at Rosemarie)
          I tried to take it back, but the
          Butcher said he gave it to her.

                    ROSEMARIE
          It's **Porter's**-house. For your face.
                (a tiny Mae)
          Fix you right up.

                    BRADDOCK
          Darling, we've got to eat this.

Jay and Howard WHOOP, fully supportive.

                    ROSEMARIE
          No! You have to put it on your
          face.

Jim looks at the boys, sighs, tilts his head back, and lays the meat over his eyes.

                    BRADDOCK
          How long do I leave it on?

Mae looks at Rosemarie who shrugs that she doesn't know.

                    JAY
          Did he fall real hard, dad?

                    BRADDOCK
          You should have seen the way he
          dropped.

                    HOWARD
          Timm-berr!

                    JAY
          Do the 'nouncer, ma. Like when we
          was little kids.

Mae smiles at him, surprised he remembers.

                    MAE
          Aren't you my little elephant?

Jim is grinning.

                    BRADDOCK
          Yeah, Mae. Do the 'nouncer,

                    MAE
          It's **An**nouncer, Jay.

But she's already moving, moving onto Jim's lap.

                    JAY
          Loud, Ma.

She has come up, starting to climb on Jim's legs.

                    MAE
          Introducing two time state Golden
          Gloves title holder...

Her VOICE is rising.

                    MAE
          ...In both the light heavyweight
          and heavyweight divisions...

She's holding eyes.

                    MAE
          ...The Bulldog of Bergen, the pride
          of New Jersey, and the hope of the
          Irish...

These last words, a final goodbye to old hopes.

                    MAE
          ...as the future champion of the
          world...
               (shouting)
          James J. Braddock!

The kids go WILD. But Jim and Mae don't notice. Something in their held gaze, an old fire, unbroken. Jim sets Mae down.

> BRADDOCK
> Wow, this really worked great.

He is up standing.

> BRADDOCK
> I feel fantastic. Let's eat.

He drops the steak SIZZLING, into the hot frying pan. The boys SHOUT, happy. Mae looks at Jim through the commotion.

> MAE
> Jim? Is it like you said? Or are
> they letting you back in?

> BRADDOCK
> No, babe. It was just one fight.

Mae, something old darkening her eyes.

90   EXT. DOCKS - MORNING   90

Jim's stands back at the gates with the familiar group. By the looks of things he's not getting picked.

> JAKE
> Six, seven, eight....

Jake spots Jim. A beat. Then the magic finger points his way.

> JAKE
> Nine.

Jim closes his eyes in relief.

91   EXT. DOCK GATES - MOMENTS LATER   91

Jim is coming through the gates. A couple of the guys notice him as he passes. Jake walks over to Jim.

> JAKE
> Listened in, last night.

> GUY
> Hey, Braddock, that really you?

> SECOND GUY
> Way to go.

Jake drops a newspaper on one of the containers. HEADLINE:
AMAZING! BRADDOCK KO'S GRIFFIN IN 3.

>   JAKE
>   Didn't think I'd be seeing you back
>   here again.

Jim shakes his head in disbelief. A few MEN crowd around.

>   BRADDOCK
>   One night only. Purse was two
>   fifty. My take's half. We owed a
>   hundred twenty. Left me five bucks.

>   JAKE
>   (laughs)
>   Makes you a rich man.
>   (serious now)
>   Good fight.

Something is stirred in these men. To come up against what
you can see and beat it back. Maybe what they all wish for.

DOCKS - WORK AREA

Jim just nods, makes his way, through back slapping, to his
place near Mike. Mike nods. They begin to work in silence.

>   MIKE
>   (finally)
>   I wouldn't have hit her.

>   BRADDOCK
>   I know, Mike -

>   MIKE
>   I couldn't have lived with myself
>   if I'd hit her.

Jim's not sure what to say.

>   MIKE
>   You get so angry with all of it,
>   you got to push somewhere. I'm
>   getting things under control.

Hook, haul, drop...

>   MIKE
>   So thanks for that.

Mike's silent nod is apology and gratitude at once.

                    MIKE
          You were going to win again, you
          could have told me.

                    BRADDOCK
          I knew, I could have bet on me too.

Mike grins.

                    MIKE
          How about you talk me through that
          last round?

Jim, a sudden, small fire in his eyes.

                    BRADDOCK
          Griffin comes out of his corner
          like a freight train, I swear...

Jim is using his right hand as he TALKS. Then, with a small
smile, switches back to his left.

92   EXT. BRADDOCK'S BLOCK - DAY   92

Mae and Rosemarie are heading home, wrapped butcher's paper
in Mae's hand. The boys play pink-ball against the ally wall.

                    MAE
          No more. Now, say it, Rosy.

                    ROSEMARIE
            (a rush)
          Don't trade daddy's autograph to
          the butcher for free meat.

Mae bites back her laugh.

                    MAE
          Why can't you ever listen to me?

Rosemarie thinks on it a bit.

                    ROSEMARIE
            (little kid serious)
          I don't know.

Mae can't help but smile. Her expression quickly darkens as
she sees Joe's familiar car pulling away from their house.

                    MAE
          Go play with the boys.

93   EXT. BRADDOCK BACKYARD - DAY   93

Jim, staring up at the sky. Mae walks out.

                    MAE
          Your daughter is now a celebrity in
          Sam's butcher shop.

Jim turns. She can see it in his eyes.

                    BRADDOCK
          Joe came by. He thinks the
          Commission might be willing to
          reverse their ruling. He thinks he
          can get me another fight.

Mae says nothing, just stares into the old fire.

                    BRADDOCK
          I'm going to stop working, get back
          into back into shape.

He's already in his pocket.

                    BRADDOCK
          Joe fronted us a $175. So I can
          train.

                    MAE
          You said it was just the one fight.

                    BRADDOCK
          It's our second chance is what it
          is. It's a chance to make you and
          the kids proud.

Mae takes a beat before going on.

                    MAE
          We got off easy when you broke that
          hand. It's not I'm not proud or
          grateful. I am. But what if
          something worse happened? And you
          can't work?

She is holding his eyes. Something she's not saying.

                    MAE
          What happens to us? To the kids
          again? We're barely managing now.

                    BRADDOCK
          Yeah, Mae. If I can't do better
          than I'm doing, we're not going to
          make it. Kill myself every day for
          a couple coins and every week we
          slip behind a little.

                    MAE
          We got out of it. We're back to
          even now. Please, baby. I'm begging
          you. We don't have anything left to
          risk.

                    BRADDOCK
          I can still take a few punches,
          Mae. And I'd rather take them in
          the ring. At least you know who's
          hitting you.

Jim smiles, turns and heads inside.

                    BRADDOCK
          Jay!

95   EXT. PARK AVENUE - MORNING   95

Mae stands before a Park Avenue apartment building, staring
up at the stone facade. TILT UP to Manhattan's silver spires.

96   INT. PARK AVENUE - ELEVATOR - MOVING   96

Mae stands, glancing nervously at the ELEVATOR OPERATOR. She
touches her tattered clothes self-consciously. WIDEN.

A well dressed MATRON stands beside Mae, offering her the
kind of gaze usually reserved for car accidents. Bad ones.

97   INT. PARK AVENUE APARTMENT BUILDING - MORNING   97

Mae comes to an apartment door. Checks a scrap of paper from
her purse. Matches the door number. She KNOCKS.

Movement inside. Motion at the key hole. Then nothing. Just
stillness beyond the portal. She KNOCKS again. Still nothing.

                    MAE
          Open the door, Joe. Joe, open the
          damn door. You're not going to hide
          in your fancy apartment and make my
          husband your punching bag all over
          again.
                    (MORE)

                        MAE (cont'd)
          We're starving and you're taking
          him from his work like some short
          little blood sucking leech and I
          won't let you get him hurt like
          that again do you hear me I will
          not let you.

That's when the door swings slightly open to reveal Joe. They
stare at each other in silence.

                        JOE
          I guess you better come in.

Joe opens the door.

A WOMAN (LUCILLE GOULD), stands in an apartment totally
empty, only high windows and wood floors. No furniture.

98   INT. GOULD APARTMENT - MOMENTS LATER   98

Joe, Mae and Lucille sit on three folding chairs in the
middle of the empty living room, sipping tea.

                        JOE
          How is it?

Joe looks at his wife who nods, smiles.

                        LUCILLE
          Too sweet per usual.

He smiles back, looks at Mae.

                        JOE
          Yours?

Mae nods. She's still off balance.

                        JOE
               (gestures to the door)
          Sorry. You just don't want folks to
          see you down is all.

                        MAE
          I didn't know. I thought....

                        JOE
          Yeah. That's the idea.
               (smiles)
          Always keep your hands up.

Mae realizes that's been Joe's saying all along.

                    JOE
          Sold the last of it two days ago.
          So Jimmy could train.

It takes Mae a moment to respond.

                    MAE
          Why?

                    JOE
          Sometimes you see something in a
          fighter. You don't even know if its
          real, you're looking for it so bad.

Joe glances out the window.

                    JOE
          You can't have no hope at all. I
          guess Jimmy's what I hope for.

Mae is startled, had no idea they shared this.

                    JOE
          He's really something, Mae.

                    MAE
          This is crazy.

No argument there.

                    MAE
          You don't even know if you can get
          him a fight, do you?

                    JOE
          I'll get him a fight. Last thing I
          do, I'll get him a fight.

But we can see that's bravado talking.

                    LUCILLE
          Honey, get us some more tea, would
          you?

Joe rises, smiling.

                    JOE
          I know who wears the pants.

He winks, goes into the kitchen. The two women sit in
silence.

                         LUCILLE
               It's not the way I imagined it
               either.

Finally, Mae who speaks.

                         MAE
               It's just that.... I hated it.
               Every day he walked out that door
               for a fight. I even hated eating
               the food it bought cause it was
               like it came right out of him.

Mae takes a beat before going on.

                         MAE
               We lost something when he stopped
               fighting. But I guess we got
               something too.

Lucille nods, her smile sad.

                         LUCILLE
               Can you ever stop yours? When he
               sets his mind to a thing.

                         MAE
               No. I wish I could. No.

                         LUCILLE
               I never know who it's harder on,
               them or us? We have to wait for
               them to fix everything. But they
               have to do it. And everyday they
               feel like they're failing us. And
               really it's just the world that's
               failed, you know?

Passing clouds dapple sunlight on wooden floors.

                         MAE
               It's...this is a lovely apartment.

                         LUCILLE
               Thank you.

The two sit together in silence, sipping tea.

101   INT. JOHNSTON'S OFFICE - DAY   101

Gould sits across the desk from Jimmy Johnston.

                    JOHNSTON
          Now what am I going to go and do
          that for?

                    JOE
          You saw the papers. News had to run
          extra copies day after Braddock's
          fight. People are sentimental.

                    JOHNSTON
          Yeah. So, tell me why I care.

                    JOE
          You're still sore over the way
          Braddock took down Griffin, fine, I
          can understand that. It was a
          heartbreak. But, look...

Joe slips two fresh, expensive cigars from his jacket, slides
one across the desk towards Johnston. And starts to sell.

                    JOE
          You got guys fighting an
          elimination series over who gets a
          shot at Max Baer for the
          Championship in June. John Henry
          Lewis is your number two in line.
          He already beat Braddock once in
          Frisco. Say you put Braddock back
          in the game against Lewis. Lewis
          wins, you get your revenge on
          Braddock, your boy's had a top
          flight tune up with full publicity
          before Lasky so what happens? You
          make more money. Now say by some
          minute, infinitesimal chance,
          Braddock beats Lewis. You got a
          sentimental favorite to go up and
          lose against Lasky and what
          happens? You make more money.
          Either way you're richer with
          Braddock back in the ring than if
          he's not. And we both know the name
          of this game...

Joe rubs fingers to thumb, the universal sign for money.

                    JOE
          And it sure as hell isn't boxing.

Johnston shakes his head in awed dismay.

JOHNSTON
They should put your mouth in a
circus.

JOE
Yeah. So what do you say?

Johnston lifts the cigar, turns it over in his hand.

101A   INT. JEANNETTE'S GYM - DAY   101A

A BOXING BAG-CLOSE. Being hit. Really, really fast. Jeannette
COACHES.

JEANNETTE
Pick it up! Come on?

102   INT. JEANNETTE'S GYM - LATER   102

FEET CLOSE. Familiar boxing shoes, Jim's shoes, dancing
around the ring.

JEANNETTE (OVER)
Okay, okay, you got your left back,
big deal, don't lock the knee, you
gotta be quicker.

TILT UP. These shoes are on George's feet, the boxer Jim
sold them to earlier.

Braddock's sparring with him, shirts dark with sweat. Mike
sits watching from the bleachers. Joe walks up to the ring.

JOE
I got you a fight.

Jim signals a stop.

JOE
You're gonna fight John Henry Lewis
again.

Braddock climbs out of the ring.

BRADDOCK
I could kiss you.

JOE
Say I was to beg you not to?

BRADDOCK
Isn't Lewis one of Johnston's boys?

                         JOE
               You let me worry about that.

                         BRADDOCK
               No wonder you won't pucker up. Bet
               you're all kissed out all ready.

Mike, unseen, has walked up to them.

                         MIKE
               Lewis? He kicked our ass in Frisco.

                         JOE
               Us? Who's this? Who's us?

                         BRADDOCK
               Hey, Mike. No shifts today?

                         MIKE
               Lewis hasn't been beat in ten
               fights.

                         BRADDOCK
               Joe Gould, Mike Wilson.

Joe looks at Mike. Starts to speak, then just shakes his
head, puts his arm around Jim and walks him off a few feet.

                         JOE
               I ain't gonna bullshit you. Right
               now you're fodder. But you win one
               and I can get you another. Win
               again and things maybe start
               getting serious.

Jim nods, then he heads towards the heavy bag.

                         JOE
               Jimmy.

Jim turns back to him. That old fire in Joe's eyes.

                         JOE
               Win.

                         BRADDOCK
                    (over his shoulder)
               Mike, come hold the bag for me.

103   INT. BUTCHER SHOP - AFTERNOON   103

Sam is weighing up some ham when the bell over the door
TINGLES. He peers over the counter and sees Rosemarie
standing there with her two stoic bodyguards.

                    ROSEMARIE
          My daddy's fighting a man who beat
          the living bjesus out of him last
          time. What kind of steaks you got?

104   INT. BRADDOCK APARTMENT - EVENING   104

Jim puts his boxing trunks in a paper bag. Stands alone a
moment, already beginning to prepare for the night ahead.

He turns to face his wife, sunset spilling into the apartment
through the low windows.

                    BRADDOCK
          I know this isn't what you wanted.

He looks down. Back up at her.

                    BRADDOCK
          But I can't win if you're not
          behind me.

                    MAE
          I'm always behind you.

She leans in and kisses him.

105   EXT. BRADDOCK APARTMENT - EVENING   105

Jim emerges into this perfect fall evening to find a few
NEIGHBORS gathered around out front.

                    NEIGHBOR
          We're rooting for you, Jim.

A familiar figure steps out of the small crowd.

                    MIKE
          How you doing, lefty?

They clasp hands.

                    BRADDOCK
          How's Sara and the baby?

                    MIKE
          It sure gives the guys a lift you
          getting back into it.

Jim shrugs it off.

                    MIKE
          Put two bucks on you, Jimmy. Don't
          let me down, now.

Braddock's expression darkens.

                    BRADDOCK
          Mike, Lewis is favored five to one.

Mike's smile is like a light. Hope, there.

                    MIKE
          How else am I gonna get rich? You
          know maybe I could come along. You
          need some help in your corner?

Jim just smiles at this outlandish request.

                    BRADDOCK
          I already got my regular seconds.
          You know how it is, huh Mike?

Jim continues on towards Joe's car waiting at the curb. Mike
watches him go.

106   INT. BOXING RING - MADISON SQUARE GARDEN - NYC - NIGHT   106

A fist snaps Jim's head back with a left. Then another. Then
another. WIDEN FURTHER...

JOHN HENRY LEWIS, black, at 6'1" and 190 pounds with a
perfect physique, rips into Jim with a series of
combinations. He's a fighter ahead of his time, fast, lethal.

                    BOND (OVER)
          Lewis the uncrowned heavyweight
          champ, having beaten Rosenbloom
          twice in nontitle fights, is here
          to repeat his Frisco performance.

His speed is dazzling. His force, impossible. But Jim is
showing surprising footwork, mounting a remarkable defense.

                    BOND
          And defeat Jim Braddock.

Jim suddenly comes in with a hard left of his own. Then another. And another. Lewis is surprised.

The rule is set, no ground will be given on either side.

107   INT. LEWIS CORNER - MOMENTS LATER   107

Lewis is breathing hard. His COACH stands over him.

> COACH
> Come on. What are you doing? You
> beat this guy easy last time.

> LEWIS
> He ain't the same guy.

108   INT. BRADDOCK CORNER - SAME MOMENT   108

Jim is slumped on his stool. Joe is trying to rub some life into Jim's arms.

> BRADDOCK
> Faster than I remember, even.

> JOE
> Yeah, he's fast. But only in one
> direction. Always moving to the
> right. Cut down the ring. You gotta
> unload. You hit him, he's not going
> to like it. The more you hit him,
> the slower he's going to get.

109   INT. RING - LATER   109

Jim and Lewis stand trading blow for blow. It's impossible that either man is still standing. Jim is on the aggressive. He stalks Lewis who dances away, now seems wary of Jim.

> BOND (V.O.)
> And they are still toe to toe, no
> one is giving an inch! I have never
> seen a fight this ferocious go on
> for this long!

Lewis knocks Jim back with a lethal combination. Jim throws a sudden uppercut. Lewis goes down on one knee.

Jim steps back.

The Ref is counting.

The crowd is ROARING.

Lewis gets up.

The Ref waves Jim in.

Jim charges back to center ring and HAMMERS Lewis again. One, two, three jabs. Lewis can't keep his guard up.

Jim goes to the body and then throws a powerful right to the head and Lewis is KNOCKED OUT OF FRAME.

The crowd EXPLODES.

JIM-CLOSE. Realizing he has won. His head is snapped back by a powerful white fist. WIDEN TO REVEAL....

110   INT. RING - MADISON SQUARE GARDEN - NYC - 1935 - NIGHT   110

Jim is now fighting Art Lasky. Lasky is moving in fast. What's dazzling about Lasky is the combination of force and endurance. Jim's landing punch after punch with no effect.

                    BOND (VO)
          After his dazzling victory against
          John Henry Lewis, the comeback of
          Jim Braddock has just hit a wall
          named Art Lasky. In the ninth...

Lasky has Jim in a corner and he is pounding bone jarring shots into Jim's ribs. Jim can't seem to find the punches before they connect. Jim strains to see the clock, endures a storm of punches to head and body. (OVER) The bell CLANGS.

Lasky walks to his corner with his hands raised in triumph!

111   INT. BRADDOCK'S CORNER - MOMENTS LATER   111

A CORNERMAN works on Jim, worse for wear. Jim stares up at the ceiling lights which suddenly drop towards him.

                    JOE
          He's a bull-rusher. He's going to
          keep doing this all night.

Jim looks up, the lights right where they should be.

                    JOE
          Where are you? Jim, this is Lasky's
          house. You got to stop him
          breathing, you get me Jim?

See something pass between them, almost a shared darkness.

                         JOE
             You hit him in the nose. You keep
             hitting him there, you get me? Make
             him bleed.

The WARNING BUZZER sounds.

                         JOE (CONT'D)
             Fill his face with blood.

112   INT. RING - LATER   112

Lasky has Jim in the corner again. Jim has his arms down, his
elbows in tight, trying to protect his ribs.

                         BOND (V.O.)
             Art Lasky is putting an end to a
             story that's been getting a lot of
             attention...

Jim has left his head completely unprotected. Lasky sees his
opening and connects flush on Jim's temple with an enormous
right hook that makes Jim spit out his mouthpiece.

The most powerful punch Lasky has. The most powerful punch
most folks in the audience have ever seen. All grow silent.

Jim just stands there, holding Lasky's eyes.

Jim doesn't fall. He turns, walks calmly across the ring and
lifts the mouthpiece.

                         BOND (OVER)
             Braddock just took Lasky's best
             punch and it didn't even phase him.
             He's showing inhuman determination.

Braddock grins, moves in on Lasky. Lasky tries to go for the
clinch but Jim gives him an upper cut, won't let him in.

113   RING - HIGH ANGLE - ONE SHOT   113

All the punches in all the coming rounds are seen in a single
flurry, hooks, jabs, clinches all one continuous bout while
(OVER) BOND clocks us through rapidly passing time.

                         BOND (OVER)
             Round thirteen...

Jim jabs from a distance; hits his nose again and again.

                         BOND (OVER)
             Round fifteen...

Jim lands THUDDING rights; goes to the body; then the face.
Lasky's nose explodes, blood everywhere.

> BOND (OVER)
> This is incredible. Braddock will
> not be denied.

Jim is on him again; a series of lethal punches sends Lasky
back, ropes the only thing keeping him up. The BELL.

BACK TO SCENE

The crowd is on it's feet. The fighters are still in the
middle of the ring.

FIND Joe looking at Jim. He offers a respectful little bow.

FIND Jim looking at Joe. He winks.

> REF
> And the winner is...

The NOISE of the crowd becomes a ROAR.

114   INT. - HOTEL HALLWAY - BRANSON MISSOURI - NIGHT   114

ANCIL HOFFMAN is running down the hallway, stops and RAPS on
a door which opens TO REVEAL a stark naked Max Baer.

> MAX
> What?

> ANCIL
> Max, Jim Braddock just beat Lasky.
> He just got to be the number one
> contender.

In the b.g. two half dressed show girls GIGGLE wildly.

> MAX
> What? I'm going to paste that guy.
> He's a chump. Why not tell his
> manager to stand him on 5th Avenue
> in front of the crosstown bus. If
> he can take that, maybe he can get
> in the ring with me. And tell
> Johnston to get somebody who can
> fight back.

> ANCIL
> You gonna bust your contract? It's
> done, Max.

Max just shuts the door in Ancil's face.

115   INT. MADISON SQUARE GARDEN - NYC - LOCKER ROOM - NIGHT   115

Jim faces Joe who's stripping his hands. (OVER) A KNOCK.

                    JOE
          I said wait! Hounds of goddamned
          hell.

                    BRADDOCK
          That's redundant by the way.

Joe shoots him a look, goes back to unwrapping.

                    JOE
          You know what this means?

                    BRADDOCK
          Don't.

                    JOE
          Not that again.

Joe's eyes turn serious. (OVER) Another KNOCK.

                    JOE
          That's three in a row, Jim. All
          contenders. You're in line again.

Remember these words. So long ago. No smiles this time.

                    BRADDOCK
          Don't, Joe. Don't jinx it.

He's serious. Shakes his head.

                    JOE
          Like before, huh?

                    BRADDOCK
          No. Last time we didn't know enough
          to be scared.

Joe pulls open the door to the now giant gaggle of REPORTERS.

                    REPORTER
          Jim, you gonna fight Max?

                    REPORTER # 2
          Do you think you can you survive in
          the ring with Baer?

Joe lets out a hungry dog HOWL. Jim can't help but grin as the Reporters engulf them both.

116   EXT.- MADISON SQUARE GARDEN - NIGHT   116

The same stage doors that Joe and Jim exited that night, so many years ago. Times have changed.

Jim's FANS are here. But gone are the flapper's dresses and dapper suits. Instead, see faces and clothes beaten rough and worn. A crowd of maybe fifty, all waiting for Jim.

So many. So hopeful. Jim stares at the crowd, stunned.

                         JOE
          You sign a few, leave em wanting.

                      BRADDOCK
          Nah, Joe. You sign em all.

He moves to them.

116A   INT. RELIEF OFFICE - DAY   116A

Jim stands in line. Someone seems to recognize him.

Jim makes it to the counter. The same Woman stands staring as he slides a familiar envelope back towards her.

                       WOMAN
          Let me get this straight?

She's looking inside the envelope, full of cash.

                       WOMAN
          You want to give it back?

117   INT. BRADDOCK APARTMENT - AFTERNOON   117

Jim ENTERS carrying a dozen roses. His smile dissolves.

Sara sits with her baby girl, her eyes red from crying. The infant has a hacking COUGH.

                        MAE
          Mike's gone missing.

Jim walks over to Mae, the kids relegated to the bedroom, straining hard to listen.

                      BRADDOCK
          How long?

> SARA
> Three days. I've been staying at my
> brother's since Jake cut him-

> BRADDOCK
> Jake? When?

> SARA
> Maybe a week after you left. You
> know how Mike gets. All his talk.
> So much trouble.

She touches her baby's face, as if she sees Mike there.

> SARA
> He's been sleeping nights down in
> the Hooverville. My brother didn't
> have room for both him and us.

She looks up at Jim.

> SARA
> Said he was doing some strategy
> work for you. He had a little cash
> coming in, down at the gym all the
> time, it made sense, you being
> friends and all.

By Sara's expression, Mae's already dashed this fantasy.

> SARA
> Last night he's supposed to meet me
> down at Quincy's. He never showed.

She's trying to keep the fear out of her VOICE.

> SARA
> Something's wrong, Jim. I know it.
> He'd never miss one of your fights.

He stares at her. Surprised by this.

> SARA
> He just wouldn't.

Sara isn't even aware that she's started to cry again.

> MAE
> Baby's got a bad cough, Jim.

Mae glances at the cash in the rainy day jar. Jim nods.

                    BRADDOCK
          You and Mae go down to Rexall, get
          something to fix her up. I'll go-

                    SARA
          I give up.

Mae and Jim, startled.

                    SARA
          What he said before he left last
          time. I should have known something
          was wrong. I give up, he said.

                    BRADDOCK
          I'm sure he's fine, Sara.

Jim. Trying to hide his lie.

                    BRADDOCK
          I'll just go round him up.

118   EXT. CENTRAL PARK WEST - SUNSET   118

     As a cab pulls away in the b.g., Jim stands on the edge of
     the park. A surreal evacuation is in progress. Under the
     watchful eyes of cops on horseback, dozens of sheep are being
     herded from the park into immense coral wagons.

119   EXT. HOOVERVILLE - SUNSET   119

     Jim winds through cardboard shanties, lit by the glow of
     trash can fires, through legions of MEN. Suits and ties sit
     around broken card tables, old furniture spitting stuffing.

     Jim approaches a MAN standing with a few others, cooking
     something over a trash can fire. Hard to tell exactly what.

                    BRADDOCK
          Excuse me.

     They look at him. Two actually tip their hats.

                    MAN ONE
          Evening, sir. Offer you a bite to
          eat. It's fresh.

     A second Man reaches forward with a bottle. Jim just shakes
     his head, smiles.

                    BRADDOCK
          I'm looking for a friend of mine.

Jim glances around. So many men, like moving shadows.

                    BRADDOCK
          Is there someone in charge?

The man just looks at him, smiles.

                    MAN ONE
          Ain't that the question of the day?

A few more cops pass, herding more sheep out towards the
street. PULL BACK AND UP as Jim heads deeper into the park,
this paper city lit by dying sun and fire, spreading on to
the steel horizon like somewhere damned.

120   INT. HOOVERVILLE - LONG NIGHT   120

                    BRADDOCK
                   (calling)
          Mike? Mike Wilson?

Smoke now billows in the distance. Several more cops race
past him, towards the growing SOUNDS of commotion ahead,
SHOUTS, angry frightened. HORSES.

                    BRADDOCK
                   (calling)
          Mike Wilson! Mike!

Pushing forward, Jim is suddenly engulfed in the center of
the CACOPHONY. The smoke here whips like flags of travelling
night, bodies run past, SHOUTS, STAMPEDING HOOVES.

                    VOICE (OVER)
          Jim. Over here. Jim.

Something races past, nearly knocking him away, two men,
being chased by a cop on horseback, almost trampling Jim.

                    BRADDOCK
          Mike?

But the figure emerging from the smoke isn't Mike at all,
just some FELLOW who looks up at him over raccoon eyes.

                    FELLOW
          Braddock, right? Seen you fight.

Jim just stares at him.

                    FELLOW
          Frank Gibson. City National. Hope
          you don't want a loan.

Jim pushes past him, through the trees and into Sheep's Meadow. This was the center of the battle, only seconds ago. A bonfire burns, Horses WHINNY on torn ground. Cops roughly gather angry men. Other men lay on the ground. Some MOAN.

Jim is looking around. A denser commotion on the fire's edge. Jim passes two COPS on horseback, one talking to his SARGENT.

> COP (OVER)
> We was just trying to clear the
> sheep, Sarge. Guys got all
> political and they charged us.

Men crowd an overturned wagon. A COP SHOOTS first one horse, then the other. Other men are moving bodies from beneath.

> COP (OVER)
> Horses got spooked, you know.
> Wagons go over.

> COP (OVER)
> Starkers just didn't get out of the
> way in time. Jesus.

Jim is moving across the fallen men. (OVER) AMBULANCES can be heard in the distance. He looks at face after face.

> VOICE
> Hey, Jim.

Jim turns. This time, it is Mike, body badly out of alignment, smile on bloody lips.

> MIKE
> You win?

Jim goes down on his knee, smoothing the hair from Mike's face, wiping blood and mud from his cheeks.

> BRADDOCK
> You're gonna be fine, Mike. You're
> gonna be okay.

Mike is in his pocket, pulls out a betting ticket with Braddock's name on it. He manages a smile.

> MIKE
> Yeah. I know it.

SMOKE blows through FRAME TO BLACK.

121   EXT. NEWARK - POTTER'S FIELD   121

A casket is lowered towards us, slowly, into the ground. Find
Mae, face wet with tears, the children at her side.

Sara, infant in her arms, stands a few feet off, taking small
comfort from Jim's WHISPERED words.

Mae, stares past her husband, to this suddenly fatherless
family's endless days ahead. She looks down.

122   INT. MADISON SQUARE GARDEN - PRESS CONFERENCE - DAY   122

Jim Joe and Mae sit at a long table facing a room of
REPORTERS. Bulbs FLASH. Mae watches from the front row.

                    REPORTER
          Frank Essex, Daily News. You got a
          lot of reporters here, you can see
          a lot of people are interested in
          this fight. You got anything to say
          to the fans, Jim?

                    BRADDOCK
          I guess-. I guess I'm grateful for
          the opportunity. Not everybody gets
          a second chance these days. I guess
          I got a lot to be grateful for.

                    REPORTER # 2
          Bob Johnson, Boston Globe. Two days
          ago we ran a story about you giving
          your relief money back. Can you
          tell our readers why?

                    BRADDOCK
          I believe we live in a country
          that's great enough to give a man
          financial help when he's in
          trouble. I've had some good fortune
          so I thought I'd return it. Let
          them give it to somebody else who
          could use it because they were good
          enough to give it to me.

                    REPORTER # 3
          Wilson Harper, AP. What's the first
          thing you're gonna do if you make
          world champion.

                    BRADDOCK
          Well I guess I gotta go out and buy
          some pet turtles. When I was
          leaving the house I told the kids I
          was going to bring home the title.
          They thought I said turtle, so
          naturally I can't let them down.

Joe LAUGHS a little too LOUD.

                    JOE
          Get the **turtle** for his kid. Cause
          of his accent, see?

                    REPORTER # 4
          John Savage, Blue Ribbon Sports.
          Baer says he's worried he's going
          to kill you in the ring. What do
          you say?

Mae can't help but look at her hands.

                    BRADDOCK
          Max Baer's the champion. I'm
          looking forward to the fight.

                    REPORTER # 5
          Jake Greenblatt, Chicago Trib. What
          changed, Jimmy? You couldn't win a
          fight for love or money. How do you
          explain your comeback?

                    BRADDOCK
          Maybe I know what I'm fighting for,
          this time around.

                    REPORTER # 5
          Yeah? What's that?

                    BRADDOCK
          I just got tired of the empty milk
          bottles is all.

A familiar figure stands, focusing on Mae.

                    SPORTY
          Sporty Lewis, New York Herald. Mrs.
          Braddock. My question is for you.
          My readers want to know, how do you
          feel about the fact that Max Baer
          has killed two men in the ring?

Mae stares at him, speechless.

> SPORTY
> Mrs. Braddock, are you scared for
> your husband's life?

> BRADDOCK
> She's scared for Max Baer is who
> she's scared for.

Jim is glaring at Sporty.

> JOE
> Okay, boys, one more. Save some
> ink for the baseball scores.

Attention returns to the Joe and Jim. But we HOLD on Mae.

123   INT. BOXING CLUB - JOHNSTON'S OFFICE - LATER   123

Old wood and enough cigar smoke to black out the noon-time
sun. Joe and Jim ENTER to find Jimmy Johnston at his desk.

> JOE
> Said downstairs you wanted to see
> us.

> JOHNSTON
> Gould. ...Jim.

> BRADDOCK
> Mr. Johnston.

Johnston lays a Daily News on the desk, opens it to the
editorial page.

> JOHNSTON
> Right here, editorial says this
> fight is good as murder and
> everyone associated with it should
> be hauled into court and prosecuted
> afterwards.

Joe says nothing.

> JOHNSTON
> Says the paper's getting all sorts
> of letters from people saying
> you're their inspiration. Like you
> saved their lives or something.

Now it's Jim's turn not to respond. Johnston begins moving
around the room, pulling the shades.

                         JOHNSTON
             You ask me, it's all crap. But if
             I'm going to promote this fight,
             I'm not getting hung out to dry if
             something happens to you.

                         JOE
             You're all heart.

                         JOHNSTON
             My heart is for my family. My balls
             and my brains are for business. And
             this is business. Got me?

Johnston turns to Jim.

                         JOHNSTON
             You will know exactly what you're
             up against and my attorney Mr.
             Mills will witness I have done
             everything in my power to warn you.

                         BRADDOCK
             I saw the Carnera fight.

Johnston moves to the projector, kills the lights. Mr. Mills
is striped with sneaking blind light.

                         JOHNSTON
             Carnera's height saved him.

                         JOE
             He was knocked down 12 times.

                         JOHNSTON
             Exactly. It would have been worse
             if he was shorter. Baer had to
             punch up to hit him which took a
             little off.

Johnston turns on the projector. The wall behind his desk
flickers. Johnston focuses the lens and we see:

ON THE WALL.

Max Baer fighting FRANKIE CAMPBELL.

                         JOHNSTON
             That's Frankie Campbell. Stand up
             fighter. Knows how to take a punch.
             His style familiar, Jim? Like
             looking in a mirror, huh?

                    JOE
          He don't need to see this.

                    JOHNSTON
          He'll see it or I'm calling off the
          fight.

Campbell steps forward with a good left jab. Baer counters
with a right, a punch with a strange and awesome power.

Campbell is spun but stays on his feet. The second punch
hammers home and Campbell collapses. He lies on the canvas,
his eyes open, a blank stare.

The Ref kneels over Campbell as his corner men scramble under
the ropes.

                    JOHNSTON
          See that combination. Campbell
          didn't go down on the first one.
          Tough guy. Second punch killed him
          on the spot.

                    JOE
          Consider your ass fully covered.
          Now cut it off will you-.

But Braddock is focused, stepping forward.

                    BRADDOCK
          Run it again.

Johnston appraises Jim, then rewinds, begins running the film
again. The same death waltz on the screen.

ON THE WALL

Baer is fighting Campbell again.

124   INT. RING - SAN FRANCISCO - BAER FIGHT   124

The fight we just saw. Campbell steps forward with that jab.
But this time it's color.

Baer counters with his right. Campbell spins, then goes down
at his feet. Eyes wide. The Ref and cornermen push in as they
lean over Campbell's lifeless body.

                    JOHNSTON (OVER)
          Autopsy said his brain was knocked
          loose from the supporting tissue.

125   INT. BOXING CLUB - JOHNSTON'S OFFICE   125

Johnston turns the lights back on.

> JOHNSTON
> Remember Ernie Schaff, stand up
> fighter, nice guy. You lost one to
> him in thirty one.

> BRADDOCK
> I remember him.

> JOHNSTON
> Ernie took one of those on the chin
> from Baer. He was dead and didn't
> know it. Next fight, first jab put
> him to sleep forever. Detached
> brain, they said.

Johnston stares at Joe and Jim.

> JOHNSTON
> Joe? No snappy comeback.

> JOE
> Guess it ain't my skull guy's going
> to try and stove in.

The way Joe looks at Jim you know what he's saying; it's okay
Jimmy, you don't have to take this fight.

> JOHNSTON
> Want to think about it?

> BRADDOCK
> You think you're telling me
> something? Sitting here with all
> the cash you need to make the right
> choice? You think triple shifts or
> working nights on the scaffolds
> ain't as likely to get a guy
> killed? How many guys got killed
> the other night just living in
> cardboard shacks to save on the
> rent money? Some guy just trying to
> feed his family. Only nobody's
> figured out a way to make a buck
> seeing how he was gonna die.

Jim's smile is fierce.

> BRADDOCK
> My profession. I'm more fortunate.

Jim is holding Johnston's eyes.

> BRADDOCK
> So, I guess I've thought about it
> all I'm going to.

> JOHNSTON
> All righty then.

He hits the lights. His duty discharged. Slides a card across
the table.

> JOHNSTON
> You guys eat here tonight. Take
> your wives. On me. We'll snap some
> pics on your way out. You change
> your mind tomorrow, least we got
> some good press out of it.

Jim has reached into his pocket, pulled out two bills and
some change. Lays them on the desk.

> BRADDOCK
> It ain't a bribe.

Johnston looks at him.

> BRADDOCK
> Two bucks ten. I already paid back
> everybody else.

Joe and Jim start to leave.

> JOHNSTON
> Jim.

Braddock turns back to face him.

> JOHNSTON
> I got reels of all Baer's fights.
> You can come up here, use the
> projector any time you want.

126   INT. THE CONTINENTAL CLUB - NIGHT   126

Still the same today. Circular. Elegant. Deco. Joe and Jim
face each other across a booth in silence.

> BRADDOCK
> Since when did you get quiet?

                    JOE
          These last three fights. We sure
          showed 'em, didn't we?

Joe looks up at him something new in his eyes.

                    JOE
          I put you in some bad situations.
          Jim, you're the toughest kid on the
          playground. But this Max Baer. It's
          a whole other thing. You got
          nothing to prove to me or anyone.

What this is. Permission. But Jim just smiles.

                    BRADDOCK
          You losing faith in me, Joe?

                    JOE
          Never. Not for one goddamn minute.

And we see it in his eyes. It's true. He never has. That's
when Lucille and Mae return from the powder room.

                    MAE
          Jimmy, can we get silver faucets?

                    BRADDOCK
          Yeah. I'll order a dozen.

Joe is already pulling something out of his back pocket. It's
a rolled up newspaper.

                    JOE
          Now, as promised, the... **piece de
          resistance.**

Joe flips open the paper dramatically.

                    JOE
          Little bird told me to check the
          evening edition. Let me see here.
               (reading)
          Boxer Jim Braddock has come back
          from the dead to change the face of
          courage in our nation...

                    BRADDOCK
          Who wrote that?

Joe smiles a you'll never believe it smile.

                         JOE
              Sporty Lewis.

Joe shakes the paper at Jim. Resumes reading.

                         JOE
              In a land that's downtrodden,
              Braddock's comeback is giving hope
              to every American. People who were
              ready to throw in the towel are
              finding inspiration in their new
              hero Jim Braddock.
                   (grinning)
              As Damon Runyon has already
              written, he's the Cinderella Man.

                         BRADDOCK
              Cinderella Man?

                         MAE
              I like it. It's girly.

                         BRADDOCK
              Oh, this is going to be fun.

The Waiter arrives, reaches in to clear. Mae's eyes dart
upwards, catching her husband's. Unspoken code.

                         MAE
              Jim.

                         BRADDOCK
              Not quite done here, friend.

As he vanishes, Mae takes a stack of napkins from her bag.
She begins folding up food scraps, putting them in her purse.

                         JOE
              I'll get the bill. Johnston's a big
              spender, he's leaving a big tip. A
              peach. Gotta love the guy.

Mae is the first to see the familiar MAN come through the
front doors, heading for the bar.

                         MAE
                   (off the door)
              Jimmy.

The GIRLS walking with him both are perfect in those days
before that term was defined by surgery.

Their escort is literally a giant. He's wearing a white fur
coat, LAUGHING through bright, white teeth. Max Baer.

> BRADDOCK
> You think Johnston set it up?

> JOE
> Sure. Few extra pics for the
> dailies.

> WAITER (OVER)
> From the gentleman at the bar.

Mae looks up to see the Waiter holding a bottle of champagne.

> WAITER
> Mr. Baer said to wish you Bon
> Voyage.

Jim is staring at Mae. The blood has run out of her face.

> JOE
> Jimmy-

> BRADDOCK
> (rising)
> Get the coats, Joe.

FAVOR Jim as he walks across to the bar. Folks notice what's
going on, go quiet, watchful.

127   INT. CONTINENTAL CLUB - BAR - SECONDS LATER   127

Jim reaches Baer who is watching him come, already rising to
greet him, all broad smiles and teeth. The men shake.

> BAER
> If it ain't Cinderella Man.

> BRADDOCK
> Thanks for the champagne, Mr. Baer.
> You keep saying in the papers how
> you're gonna kill me in the ring.
> You know I have three little kids.
> You're upsetting my family.

Max leans in, close, his tone unexpected.

> BAER
> Listen to me Braddock, I'm asking
> you sincerely not to take this
> fight. People admire you.
> (MORE)

                              BAER (cont'd)
                    You seem like a decent fellow. I
                    really don't want to hurt you.

Max is staring down into Jim's eyes. He really is concerned.

                              BAER
                    Its no joke, pal. People die in
                    fairy tales all the time.

That's when both of them are illuminated by photo flashes.

                              VOICE'S
                    Max! Jim! Max!

A FEW PHOTOGRAPHERS have rushed in from outside, now SNAPPING
shots of the two. Baer disengages, suddenly all LOUD bravado.

                              BAER
                    You know I was thinking, smart
                    thing would be to take a fall.
                    Circus act's over, old man.

Jim locks eyes with Baer.

                              BRADDOCK
                    I think I'll try going a few rounds
                    with the dancing bear.

                              JOE
                    That's a good one. Okay. Let's keep
                    it in the ring.

Joe has arrived. Mae and Lucille stand not far behind him.
Baer's eyes grow lethal.

                              BAER
                    You should talk to him, lady. You
                    are sure too pretty to be a widow.

The two Girls TITTER.

                              JOE
                         (to Jim)
                    Simmer down!

                              BAER
                    On second thought, maybe I can
                    comfort you after he's gone.

Joe's leaps for Baer like a tiny, rabid dog, Jim barely
stopping him by the waist.

Mae grabs Baer's Martini off the bar and sends it SPLASHING,
into his face.

A storm of flash bulbs from the photographers.

                    BAER
          You get that boys? He's got his
          wife fighting for him.

The moment lasts, frozen in time, Jim and Max just staring at
each other down. Then Jim smiles at Baer.

                    BRADDOCK
          Yeah. She's sure something, ain't
          she?

Jim nods, and as Jim's group heads out, Baer catches Mae's
eyes. He smiles, the air still crackling with tension.

128   INT. BASEMENT APARTMENT - NIGHT   128

Jim still wears his suit, on his knees, boxing with the boys.
Mae is at the sink, scrubbing a pan with steel wool.

                    BRADDOCK
               (demonstrating)
          Never take your eyes off your
          opponent. Always follow me.

                    MAE
               (not turning)
          That's enough, now.

Jim glances up at Mae.

                    BRADDOCK
          There's more than one fighter in
          the Braddock family, tell you that.

                    HOWARD
          What about the left, Dad?

Jay feints a straight jab at Howard.

                    JAY
          Like that?

                    MAE
               (shouting)
          I said enough, Jay Braddock.

All turn to her, stunned. She stares at them a beat.

                    MAE
          No boxing in the house, no boxing
          out of the house.
               (MORE)

                    MAE (cont'd)
          No boxing, period. You are going to
          stay in school, then college, you
          are going to have professions, you
          are not going to get your skulls
          smashed in, is that clear?

And with that she is gone, out the back door.

129   EXT. BRADDOCK BASEMENT APARTMENT - NIGHT   129

Mae stands with her back to him as Jim emerges.

                    MAE
          I used to pray for you to get hurt.

Jim is startled.

                    MAE
          Just enough so you couldn't fight
          anymore.

Jim is speechless.

                    MAE
          And when they took your licence,
          even scared as I was, I went to the
          church and thanked God for it. I
          always knew a day might come where
          it could kill you. I just knew. And
          now it's here.

                    BRADDOCK
          You're just getting the jitters.

                    MAE
          There's more to it. We've got
          enough now. Why can't you stop?
          He's killed two men, Jim. What's
          worth it?

                    BRADDOCK
          This is what I know how to do.

He's looking at her, trying to find the right words.

                    BRADDOCK
          I have to believe I have some say
          over our lives, see? That
          sometimes, I can change things. If
          I don't, its like I'm dead already.

                    MAE
          I need you to be safe. So much.

                    BRADDOCK
          Mae. Nothing's safe anymore.

She just stares at him.

                    MAE
          I stood by until now. For all of
          it. But not for this, Jim. I just
          can't. So, you train, all you want.
          Make a show of it for yourself, for
          the papers. But you find a way out
          of that fight. Break your hand
          again if you have to. But if you
          set foot out of this door to fight
          Max Baer I won't be behind you
          anymore.

130   INT. GYM - MORNING   130

Jim is sitting in the corner wearing a flak jacket, his
expression dark. Joe stands with Jeannette.

                    JOE
          What's wrong with him?

Jeannette shrugs. Watches Braddock a beat.

                    JOE
          So, how's he doing?

                    JEANNETTE
          He's old, he's arthritic and his
          ribs aren't right since Lasky.

Somebody comes up, WHISPERS in Joe's ear. Joe nods.

                    JOE
          Press is here. Peel that rig off or
          Baer'll see you got a rib problem.

Braddock nods warily. Strips off his flak jacket. Heads for
the ring where George waits.

131   INT. BRADDOCK APARTMENT - DAY   131

Mae stands over a newspaper spread flat on the kitchen table.
Her expression is dark, closed.

The door swings open and Jim ENTERS from the gym. He looks up
at her. Tension here as, wordlessly, she turns to the stove.

Jim crosses to the table.

132   EXT. BRADDOCK APARTMENT - AFTERNOON   132

Jim lifts Howard by the belt, kisses his head, leans down to
kiss Jay. He takes Rosy in a hug, sweet hair in his face.

Finally he rises to Mae. A taxi waits. More neighbors stand
around this time. She leans up and kisses him softly on the
lips.

                    BRADDOCK
          I can't win if you're not behind
          me.

                    MAE
          Then don't go, Jimmy.

The moment lasts. Then Mae turns. Jim watches as Mae leads
the kids away, down the block.

134   INT. TAXI - NYC - DRIVING - AFTERNOON   134

As the car pulls up to the garden, masses of people crowd the
box office. Men and women. Old and young alike. Jim sits
staring through his own reflection at the crowd in stunned
silence. (OVER) An EXPLOSION of VOICES AND SOUND.

136   INT. ALICE'S HOUSE - NEWARK - LATE AFTERNOON   136

The kids spill in. Mae stands in the door facing her sister.

                    MAE
          No radio, Alice.

Alice nods.

                    MAE
          I'll be back soon.

Alice watches her go.

137   INT. BAER'S DRESSING ROOM - MAGIC HOUR   137

Decked out like a movie star's. Photos of Baer with various
celebrities. Max watches film of Lasky breaking Jim's ribs.

                    MAX
          You get it there like I told you?

Max's Manager Ancil stands not far off.

                    ANCIL
          Yeah.

                         MAX
                    You sure?

                         ANCIL
                    It's at the back gate, Max, Jeez, I
                    checked myself.

                         MAX
                    That's all I can do for him.

138   EXT. BEHIND THE GARDEN - CONTINUOUS   138

An AMBULANCE and CREW waiting vigil.

139   EXT. CHURCH - MAGIC HOUR   139

Mae walks across the church yard. People are streaming in.
Odd for this time of day. Father Rorick is at the door.

                         MAE
                       (puzzled)
                    Father?

                         FATHER RORICK
                    Hello, Mae.

                         MAE
                    I came to pray for Jim.

He smiles at her.

                         FATHER RORICK
                    You too?

He pushes open the door. The church is full. Packed. Hundreds
of people there in prayer.

                         FATHER RORICK
                    So have they.

                         MAE
                    I don't-

She stares at the full pews.

                         FATHER RORICK
                    Maybe sometimes people need to see
                    someone do it so they can do it
                    themselves.

Rows and rows of people, all on their knees.

> FATHER RORICK
> They think he's fighting for them.

As Mae looks at the people all there for Jim. PUSH IN ON Mae as maybe, for the first time. She understands.

140   INT. QUINCY'S BAR   140

Folks are gathering around a radio.

141   INT. BUTCHER SHOP - EVENING   141

Sam comes from behind the counter, glances up at an autographed photo of Jim. Hangs the closed sign as he EXITS.

142   EXT. STREET - EVENING   142

A small group of men stand under a lighted window as SAM comes to join them. From inside a RADIO can be heard.

PULL BACK AND UP as we see similar groups of men and women, gathered up and down the block by open windows, listening.

143   INT. JIM'S DRESSING ROOM - NIGHT   143

Joe is taping up Jim's hands. Jim seems far away. A heavy air permeates the room. All this is suddenly too real.

> JOE
> Who beat John Henry Lewis?

Jim smiles. The old game.

> BRADDOCK
> That would have been me.

> JOE
> Who whupped Lasky?

> BRADDOCK
> As far as I can tell that would
> have been me too.

> JOE
> Who-

A KNOCK at the door. It opens. A small, familiar form stands there. Joe can't help but half smile.

> JOE
> I'll tell you **that's** a bet I
> shoulda taken-

                    BRADDOCK
          Joe...

Joe looks up as Jim puts his finger to his lips.

                    JOE
          Shhh.

Joe smiles. Nods slightly to Mae.

                    JOE
          Scuse me a minute.

Joe slips past her. Husband and wife stand there staring at
each other.

                    MAE
          You can't win without me behind
          you.

                    BRADDOCK
          That's what I keep telling you.

His eyes are shining. Maybe tears. Maybe just the light.

                    MAE
          Thought it looked like rain, you
          know? Used what was in the jar.

She lifts a brown paper bag. Hands it to him.

                    MAE
          Maybe I understand some.

He opens the package. In the bag, a new pair of boxing shoes.

                    MAE
          About having to fight.

Tears are streaming down her face.

                    MAE
          I don't know what I was saying. I'm
          always behind you Jimmy. So you
          just you remember who you really
          are.

Her smile snaps your heart.

>   MAE
> You're the Bulldog of Bergen, the
> pride of New Jersey, your wife's
> hope and your kids hero and you're
> the champion of my heart James J.
> Braddock.

Jim stands taping his hand, his eyes so strong with love.

>   BRADDOCK
> You better get home. Boxer's hang
> around places like this and you
> don't wanna get tangled up with
> that crowd. Nice girl like you.

>   MAE
> See you at home, okay? Please,
> Jimmy. See you at home.

Brave despite her fear.

>   BRADDOCK
> See you at home.

144   INT. MSG BOWL - BEHIND THE BACK ROW - NIGHT   144

As Jim emerges into the smoke of the Garden, the crowd is
talking in WHISPERS.

As Jim steps into the aisle, he looks around, disturbed by
the quiet. What he sees haunts him.

145   INT. MSG BOWL - THE CROWD - NIGHT   145

The cheap seats are filled with PEOPLE wearing their best
shabby clothes.

PEOPLE who look as if they could stand a good meal.

PEOPLE from the street, from the basements.

>   JOE
>   (stunned)
> God Almighty.

Jim is moved beyond words, begins one of the strangest walks
that any boxer has ever taken into the ring.

As he passes, people get to their feet and stare at him. Soon
the whole Garden is on their feet, silently watching.

After what feels like an eternity, someone shouts Jim's name.

146   EXT. STREET - CONTINUOUS   146

Sam and a now larger group quiet as the radio in the window
comes to life with a BUZZ.

147   INT. FATHER RORICK'S CHURCH - CONTINUOUS   147

A radio is set up in the sanctuary. Father Rorick's prayers
are interrupted as his radio begins to WHINE.

Sara jumps, startled. The baby CRIES.

149   EXT. MADISON SQUARE GARDEN BOWL - L.I.C. - CONTINUOUS   149

Those who couldn't get in crowd around speakers that SCREAM.

150   INT. ALICE'S HOUSE - CONTINUOUS   150

Alice opens the closet door to see that the children have
dragged the radio into the dark, listening to the ROAR.

Alice sees the desperation in their faces as they stare up at
her, the VOICE on the radio trying to cut through the NOISE.

                    BOND (V.O.)
          I don't know if you can hear me out
          there. I can't hear myself. Madison
          Square Garden is on its feet and
          the noise is deafening!

151   INT. MSG BOWL - CONTINUOUS   151

Jim, nearing the ring, stunned at the EXPLOSION of HOLLERING
and STAMPING that is going on all around him.

152   INT. RINGSIDE - CONTINUOUS   152

Bond is literally YELLING into the microphone!

                    BOND (V.O.)
          We saw people lining up to buy
          tickets tonight who looked as if
          they were spending their last
          dollar. But they're here now, and
          35,000 strong. Listen to them!

Bond holds up the microphone.

153   INT. RING - CONTINUOUS   153

Jim climbs into the ring and looks around at the crowd,
clearly overwhelmed. The crowd ROARS at him.

154   INT. MSG BOWL - BEHIND THE BACK ROW - CONTINUOUS   154

Max stands listening to the ROARING crowd, a shade of
jealousy darkening his face. Finally, he smiles, taps Ernie
on the shoulder, and Ernie heads up the aisle.

155   INT. THE RING - CONTINUOUS   155

A wave of respectful silence begins to roll toward the ring
from the back of the Garden.

Jim sees Max Baer headed toward the ring.

By the time Max is halfway up the aisle, the Garden is nearly
stilled again.

AISLE - CONTINUOUS

The silence does not bother Max. He eats it up.

THE RING - CONTINUOUS

By the time Max climbs into the ring, he is intense to the
point of arrogance. He glares at Jim. Jim glares back.

156   INT. RINGSIDE - PRESS ROW - CONTINUOUS   156

Sporty Lewis climbs over the feet of the other reporters.

157   INT. RING - LATER   157

MAX'S GLARE-CLOSE. PULL BACK TO REVEAL...

Referee JOHNNY McAVOY has called the fighters and their
cornermen into center ring for their final INSTRUCTIONS.

                    GARY
          One minute to midnight, Cinderella!

                    JOE
          Your clock's about ticked out,
          asshole.
               (to Ancil)
          You watch your boy.
               (to the ref)
          You hear that, Mac, tell that
          shmuck none of that manhandling.

                    ANCIL
          Shut up.

                    MAX
          You gonna let this prick run off
          his mouth like that?

                    JOE
          Hey. Look it can talk. Max, you're
          cuter than a shit house rat but get
          the hell outta here.

                    MCAVOY
          All right, all right.

Through it all, Jim has been perfectly still, silent.

                    MCAVOY
          I want you to break clean. I don't
          want you to hold and hit or hit on
          the breakaway. Now shake hands and
          come out fighting. Keep your
          punches up. Go to your corners.

Joe starts to hurl a response. Instead, just shakes his head.

158   INT. RING - MOMENTS LATER   158

The crowd is deathly quiet. Jim, in his corner, poised, calm.
His eyes are closed. He might just be praying.

                    JOE
          You can do this. This guy's made
          for you. Have a picnic.

Jim doesn't even smile.

159   INT. RINGSIDE - CONTINUOUS   159

Bond is now almost whispering.

                    BOND
          Jim Braddock's rise from soup lines
          to number one heavyweight contender
          has truly been miraculous. Now,
          never in all my years, have I seen
          the arena so quiet.

The BELL rings.

160   INT. RING - ROUND ONE - CONTINUOUS   160

Jim attacks, landing a hard right to Max's face that brings
the crowd to their feet.

Max grins from ear to ear. Jim sticks him again and this time Max clinches.

> MAX
> (as to a naughty child)
> Now, now.

McAvoy separates them.

Jim has good footwork going, changes direction, goes at Baer again. Baer blocks Jim's jabs by swatting them with his right like flies. Jim keeps coming and they clinch.

> BAER
> Calm down, old man. I'll let the
> fight go a few rounds.

The Ref separates them. Jim hits Max again, this time a right, and Max smiles with great indulgence and dances away.

160A   INT. BRADDOCK'S CORNER - CONTINUOUS   160A

Jim sits INTO FRAME.

> JOE
> Okay, you got him, he don't know
> what he bought into. You're taking
> the guy to school, baby. Just keep
> him turning. You're a godamned
> gazelle, Jimmy. Use that left.

161   INT. RINGSIDE PRESS ROW - ROUND TWO   161

Bond and the other reporters are baffled.

> BOND
> A fight that no one expected to go
> one round has gone 2 but only
> because Max Baer is toying with
> Braddock, there is no other word
> for it. He's hardly thrown a punch
> and is laughing at Braddock's every
> strike.

162   INT. RING - CONTINUOUS   162

Max moves around the ring, throwing light jabs.

Max has a habit of wiping his glove on the back of his trunks after he lands a punch. It looks as if he doesn't like his opponent's sweat on it.

Jim is stalking Max but to little avail.

Max grooms himself between punches, making sure his trunks are straight, his hair in place.

Finally Jim lands a good stiff jab and Max wobbles his legs as if he is about to go down.

Jim comes after him.

With shocking ferocity and speed, Max lands an explosive right to Jim's ribs that knocks the breath out of him.

Jim counters and the two explode into a flurry of punches, then finally clinch. Baer hits him dead in the bad ribs.

                    BAER
          That the right spot, old man.

By Jim's agonized look and his sharp GASP for air, it is. The BELL rings.

163   INT. BRADDOCK'S CORNER - MOMENTS LATER   163

Joe pulls on the waistband of Jim's trunks to help him breathe. Ray pours water in Jim's mouth but he coughs it up.

                  BRADDOCK
          Air!

                  JOE
          Don't talk about it. Just breath
          it. Deep breath.

The WARNING BUZZER.

164   INT. RING - ROUND FIVE   164

Jim is actually controlling the round, repeatedly jabbing Max. Jim's footwork has never been quicker.

                  MAX
          I'm getting bored, old man.

Max throws a series of punches, landing one below the belt.

                  BRADDOCK
          Keep em up, Max.

Max lands a stunning combination to Jim's head.

                  MAX
          That up enough?!

                    BRADDOCK
            Yeah, Max. That's fine.

Max comes at Jim, hard, but Jim slips his right, making Max
look awkward and the crowd BOOS. Max is not pleased.

                    MAX
            How's that wife of yours?

Max clinches Jim and SMACKS him with an illegal back hand. In
the b.g Joe jumps up and begins SHOUTING.

                    JOE
            What the Hell, McAvoy? Wake up you
            wet son of a bitch, wake up.

                    MAX
            She talk about me?

But Jim is still coming, landing jabs. Max pulls Jim into a
clinch and Jim slyly head butts Max.

Max is pissed, throws Jim against the ropes and the crowd
explodes in tremendous BOOING.

                    MAX
            She say my name in her sleep?

Max salutes the crowd contemptuously, sticks his glove in
Jim's face.

                    MAX
            She miss me?

Jim evades and scores. Max has tied Jim up in the corner.

                    JOE
            You want to fight him or fuck him?

Max shoots Joe a glare.

                    BAER
            That's your job, assh-

WHAM. Jim scores a jab. Then another. Then a third.

                    BRADDOCK
            No, Max. She don't miss you.

(OVER) the BELL.

165   INT. MAX'S CORNER - LATER   165

Ernie Goins works over Max.

                    ANCIL
          What are you doing?

                    MAX
          Don't worry about it.

                    ANCIL
          Then quit screwing around.

Max gives Ernie a look that shuts him up.

                    MAX
          Relax.

166   INT. RING - ROUND SEVEN   166

(OVER) The BELL. Max has had his fun. As he moves out from
his corner, he is all business.

From below Jim's corner, Joe sees the look on Max's face and
screams at Jim.

                    JOE
          He's comin', he's comin'!
               (to himself)
          Shit.
               (shouting again)
          Keep sliding, keep sliding to the
          right!

THE CROWD'S POV

The crowd senses the change in Baer and they sweep to their
feet in quiet alarm. Jim goes right at him and the two
fighters explode into a clash in the middle of the ring.

They see Jim throw a good jab, only to have Max fire with the
right that just misses.

There is a collective intake of BREATH in the crowd.

THE RING - CONTINUOUS

Max charges hard, lethal. He dogs Jim relentlessly.

                    BAER
          Yeah, run, hobble away.

He catches him, now, a short, powerful right. Here is the
Champion we saw take Carnera down.

                    BAER
          Not fast enough, grandpa.

Jim is hurt, but manages a jab that snaps Max's head way
back. Then Jim clinches.

As the bell CLANGS, Max pushes the Ref out of the way,
switches his momentum to the right and lands a series of
combinations on Jim. Jim recovers with a powerful upper cut
and left hook. Both men just stare at each other.

166A   INT. BRADDOCK'S CORNER - CONTINUOUS   166A

Joe stands over Jim.

                    JOE
          You got all your ugly friends down
          from Jersey dressed up nice come
          out to see you, now you're putting
          'em to sleep. You're not turning
          him anymore. Pick it up, Jim. Be
          the boss, here.

167   INT. ALICE'S HOUSE - LATER   167

Mae has entered to find her sister and children all at the
open closet door. Alice glances up, riveted but guilty.

                    ROSEMARIE
          It's the cops.

                    BOND (V.O.)
          Braddock has fought better than
          anybody thought he could but some
          would say that it is only because
          Baer has allowed it.

(OVER) The BELL signals the tenth round.

                    JAY
          Please, Ma.

Mae stares a beat. Then she walks into the living room,
unable to listen.

168   INT. QUINCY'S BAR - LATER   168

The guys are all frozen and seem not to be breathing as:

> BOND (V.O.)
> Oh! What a tremendous shot by Baer,
> flush on Braddock's chin!

169   EXT. STREET - CONTINUOUS   169

Sam and crowd, horror flooding Sam's face.

> BOND (V.O.)
> Braddock is reeling against the
> ropes while Baer stands like a wood
> chopper waiting for the tree to
> fall!

170   INT. RING - ROUND TEN - CONTINUOUS   170

Jim sags against the ropes but does not go down.

Baer is surprised. Finally he shrugs and moves in to clean up
the mess he has made of Jim.

Jim pushes off the ropes and half staggers out to meet Max.
He lands a sharp jab that takes Max completely off guard.

Digging all the way down in the well, Jim follows the jab
with another, and another.

Startled, Max steps back and wipes the blood bursting from
his lip into his glove.

Then, as is his habit, Max wipes his glove on his trunks. And
Jim sees it. An opening.

Jim steps in and nails him with an EXPLOSIVE right hand.

Max staggers further back, reeling and insulted that someone
would interrupt his ritual.

Frustrated and angry, Max lunges with looping rights, missing
again and again.

And with each miss, Jim stabs Max with a jab, infuriating the
Champ even more.

The fighters can't hear the BELL, the crowd is so LOUD.
Johnny McAvoy has to pull them apart.

171   INT. BRADDOCK'S CORNER - MOMENTS LATER   171

Ray is working on a cut spreading beneath Jim's eye. Joe
looks into Jim's eyes and at the cut on his cheek.

JOE (CONT'D)
Jimmy, win, lose, or draw...

Joe looks near tears.

BRADDOCK
Thanks, Joe. For all of it.

Joe starts to answer. Jim's smile is impossibly warm

BRADDOCK
Joe. Stop talking.

Joe smiles back. The WARNING BUZZER sounds.

172   INT. ALICE'S HALLWAY - CONTINUOUS   172

Mae is against the wall near the closet. Listening.

BOND
James J. Braddock coming out for
the 12th round is showing this
crowd what heart is all about.

173   INT. RING - ROUND TWELVE   173

Max sticks his left hand into Jim's face, not to throw a
punch, but so he cannot see the vicious right hand coming
It's a trademark Max Baer move.

But Jim has seen it. He slaps the left aside and stings Max
with a jab. Max is not in any way amused.

Jim moves fast, slips a Baer punch and lands two more jabs.
Baer holds his arm out to Jim's face, blocking him.

Jim fakes Baer and lands a couple more sharp punches. Max
goes for the clinch and hits Jim in the ribs.

Max backhands Jim as the Ref separates them. But Jim finds a
the gap and scores two more punches.

174   INT. THE CROWD - CONTINUOUS   174

The crowd is nearly numb with anticipation and disbelief.

175   INT. RINGSIDE PRESS ROW - CONTINUOUS   175

Even the Reporters are in shock.

SPORTY
Am I seeing what I'm seeing?

Sporty Lewis jumps up, a little out of control. The crowd
rouses and starts SCREAMING at the ring!

                    CROWD
          Braddock! Braddock!

176   INT. THE RING - CONTINUOUS   176

Out of pure frustration, Max suddenly charges and hits Jim
with another left way below the belt.

Jim doubles up as the bell CLANGS.

Joe is over the ropes, going straight for Max.

                    JOE
          Why don't you just kick him in the
          balls, you asshole!

McAvoy intercepts Joe and hauls him, SHOUTING, back across
the ring.

                    JOE
          Let me have a shot at him, you son
          of a bitch!

177   INT. MAX'S CORNER - CONTINUOUS   177

Johnny McAvoy comes over and points at Max. Max has a cut and
a knot on his head.

                    MCAVOY
          That last low blow will cost you
          the round, Max.

Max waves him away. Ernie gets into Max's face.

                    ANCIL
          You're behind. Are you listening to
          me? You wanna lose the goddamn
          championship to this nobody?

Max shoves Ernie aside.

                    ANCIL (CONT'D)
          Put him down!

177A   INT. BRADDOCK'S CORNER - CONTINUOUS   177A

Mcavoy crosses through the corner.

                    MCAVOY
          Last round.

                    JOE
          That's right. Next champ.
               (back to Jim)
          Look you won this. It's a cinch. Be
          cagey. I know you don't like laying
          back. But you stay away from his
          right. I mean it Jim.

Braddock just stares.

                    JOE
          You hearing me? In and out. Lay
          back.

178   INT. RING - ROUND FIFTEEN   178

The two boxers explode out of their corners like colliding
freight trains. Baer's punches are furious, lethal.

179   INT. ALICE'S APARTMENT - NIGHT   179

Mae walks into the closet to stand with her family.

                    BOND
          In the fifteenth and final round
          they are yelling for Braddock to
          stay away because Baer is going for
          the knockout! But Braddock will
          give no quarter. He just keeps
          coming.

180   EXT. STREET - CONTINUOUS   180

Sam and the listening group are breathless.

                    BOND (V.O.)
          Baer is delivering the biggest
          punches of the fight, maybe of his
          life! But Braddock is not only
          standing, he is moving forward!

181   INT. RINGSIDE - CONTINUOUS   181

The crowd from the cheap seats has surged forward, stamping
and SCREAMING, pinning Joe and everyone ringside against the
edge of the canvas. Joe is YELLING his lungs out!

                    JOE
          Take a walk, Jimmy!

Sporty Lewis and the other reporters press the ring. Bond is
on his feet, yelling into the microphone in his hand.

                    BOND
        This is not boxing, folks! This is
        a Walloping Ballet!

182   INT. RING - CONTINUOUS   182

      Jim and Max are both knotted, bloodied, and snuffing like
      winded horses.

      But who is stalking whom?

      Max is sailing punches, every last one of them a knockout.
      Except Jim is still standing. And coming with his beloved
      left jab.

      These seconds are an eternity for the two of them. There is
      no other place, no other time, only now, this, forever.

      Jim lands a series of Jabs. But he's open, only an instant,
      turned slightly towards the ropes. All Max needs.

      Max delivers a powerful right that spins Jim around.

      Max initiates the second part of his lethal combination. A
      right uppercut that seems to start from below the floor.

      This is the blow that kills him.

      All goes silent.

      FACES IN THE CROWD. Frozen terror.

183   INT. THE BAR - CONTINUOUS   183

      They know.

184   INT. CHURCH - CONTINUOUS   184

      Sara stares up at the silent radio. All hope gone.

185   EXT. STREET - CONTINUOUS   185

      Sam SMASHES his hand on the building wall, turns away.

187   INT. ALICE'S HOUSE - NEWARK - CONTINUOUS   187

      The children look up at Mae, eyes wet with terror.

188   INT. RING - CONTINUOUS   188

      Jim's death. Frozen in time.

      But Jim has decided to die another day.

Jim avoids the right, pivots and counters with a couple of
hard lefts.

As Max practically jumps onto his shoes, Jim smashes an
uppercut that brings Max to his toes.

They stand there in center ring as if chained together and
trade punches.

And someone is pulling them apart, away from the center of
the world, into the madhouse that is erupting around them.

189   INT. ALICE'S HOUSE - CONTINUOUS   189

                         BOND (V.O.)
                It's over, the fight is over, and
                the referee is pulling them apart!

Mae covers her mouth to stifle her SOBS of relief.

190   INT. RINGSIDE - CONTINUOUS   190

Sporty Lewis yanks furiously on McAvoy's trouser leg. McAvoy
tries to shake him off but Lewis won't let go.

                         MCAVOY
                What?!

                         SPORTY
                How'd you score it, Johnny?

                         MCAVOY
                9. 5. 1 even.

                         SPORTY
                Even?

191   INT. CHURCH - CONTINUOUS   191

People stare at the radio in the sanctuary.

                         BOND (V.O.)
                The crowd, on its feet for almost
                the entire fight is still standing,
                yelling for who they clearly
                believe to be the winner of this
                fight...

192   INT. CORNER - CONTINUOUS   192

Jim stands in the corner as Joe pulls the laces out of his
gloves. Jeanette tries to stop the flow of blood from his
deep cut. Joe keeps looking at the Judges.

                         JOE
            I don't like it, Jimmy. Every time
            they take this long for a decision
            they're deciding to screw somebody.

Max suddenly appears. Joe glares at him. Max looks Jim in the
eye, leans in close so he can be heard over the crowd.

                         MAX
            You beat me. No matter what they
            say.

Jim starts to say something but Max is already walking away.

193   INT. RINGSIDE PRESS ROW - CONTINUOUS   193

Sporty Lewis is standing at the corner of the ring.

                         SPORTY
            They're robbing him.

The crowd starts YELLING for a decision and STAMPING on the
floor until it sounds like THUNDER in the Garden.

194   INT. RING - CONTINUOUS   194

A silver microphone drops from the ceiling to the center of
the ring. Ring Announcer, AL FRAZIN, enters the ring.

The NOISE of the crowd falls quickly away.

THE CROWD - CONTINUOUS

35,000 people standing together in gradations of light.

RING - CONTINUOUS

Frazin taps the microphone and the Garden is so quiet that it
sounds like someone throwing rocks at the walls.

                         FRAZIN
            Ladies and Gentlemen! I have your
            decision!

Frazin squints and studies the card in his hand.

                         FRAZIN (CONT'D)
            Winner...
                 (looks at the card again)
            ...and NEW Heavyweight Champion
            of...

The words are drowned out by an explosion of noise!

195   EXT. ALICE'S HOUSE - CONTINUOUS   195

Mae's SCREAM echoes down the block!

196   INT. ALICE'S HOUSE - LIVING ROOM - CONTINUOUS   196

The kids spring from the closet and hop about the living room
as if on pogo sticks as Mae and Alice embrace.

197   EXT. NORTH BERGEN STREETS - CONTINUOUS   197

People pour from their houses, YELLING the news as SIRENS
roar!

199   INT. QUINCY'S BAR - CONTINUOUS   199

Quincy is pouring free beer into the rioting crowd. A bunch
of very tough men are CRYING like babies.

202   INT. CHURCH - CONTINUOUS   202

Sara, baby in arms, closes her eyes, spilling silent tears.

Father Rorick bows his head, unable to completely hide his
wry, satisfied smile. He glances skyward.

                    FATHER RORICK
          Thank you.

202A   INT. ALICE'S HOUSE - CONTINUOUS   202A

All hysterical save Rosy, who smiles, perfectly calm.

                    ROSEMARIE
          It's the meat.

203   INT. RINGSIDE PRESS ROW - CONTINUOUS   203

The Reporters are all pushing and shoving, trying to get out
of the crowd to file their stories.

Sporty Lewis sits by himself, staring up at the ring, his
arms across his chest, a half smile on his lips, reliving the
fight, the miracle. In no hurry to go.

204   INT. RING - CONTINUOUS   204

Max is hemmed into his corner and cannot escape through a
crowd that will not go home.

Joe actually grabs Johnston and hugs him, unable to help
himself, bathing in this once in a lifetime moment.

Jim stands in the center of the ring, his arm raised in victory, tears flowing from his eyes, but with a look on his face, as if his mind is somewhere else.

PULL BACK AND UP now, time and color bleeding away one last time, higher still until this image HOLDS, frozen.

FINAL FADE TO BLACK

STILLS

Russell Crowe as Jim Braddock and Renée Zellweger as Mae, his wife

Russell Crowe as Jim Braddock

Renée Zellweger as Mae Braddock

Paul Giamatti as Joe Gould

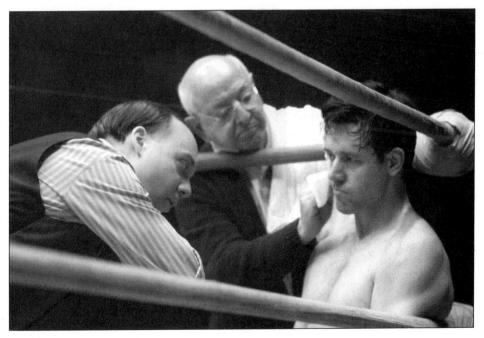

Joe Gould (Paul Giamatti) in the corner with Jim Braddock (Russell Crowe) and
Angelo (Angelo Dundee)

Jim Braddock (Russell Crowe) with his three children, left to right, Howard (Patrick Louis), Rosemarie (Ariel Waller), and Jay (Connor Price)

Jim Braddock (Russell Crowe) talking with his son Jay (Connor Price)

Jim Braddock (Russell Crowe) down at the longshoremen's line

Mae (Renée Zellweger) gets notified about the electricity being turned off.

Mae (Renée Zellweger) and Jim (Russell Crowe) before the big fight

Mae (Renée Zellweger) and Jim Braddock (Russell Crowe) doing prefight publicity.

Max Baer (Craig Bierko), Jim Braddock (Russell Crowe), and Joe Gould (Paul Giamatti) encounter each other at a restaurant before the big fight.

Jim Braddock (Russell Crowe) kidding around with his daughter Rosemarie
(Ariel Waller)

Jim Braddock (Russell Crowe) and Joe Gould (Paul Giamatti) concerned about
the fighter's hand

Joe Gould (Paul Giamatti) yelling encouragement to Jim Braddock (Russell Crowe)

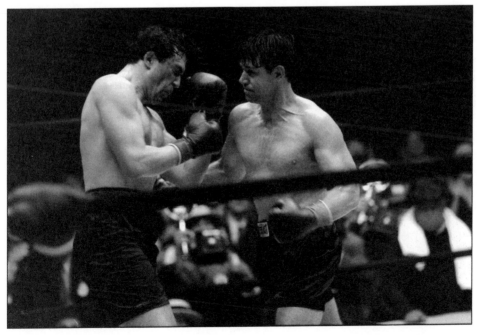

The big fight—Jim Braddock (Russell Crowe) vs. Max Baer (Craig Bierko)

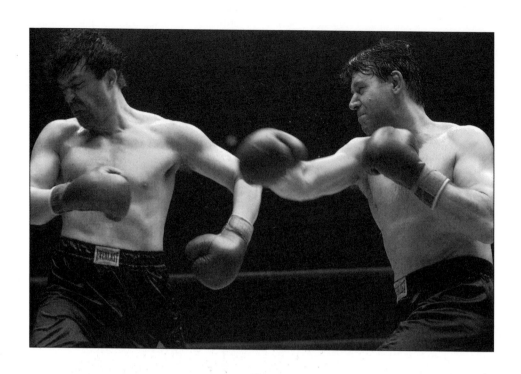

Jim Braddock (Russell Crowe) takes on the champ Max Baer (Craig Bierko).

The new champion Jim Braddock (Russell Crowe)

The winner is mobbed by reporters and well-wishers.

Russell Crowe and Ron Howard

Ron Howard, Connor Price, and Russell Crowe

Renée Zellweger, Russell Crowe, and Ron Howard

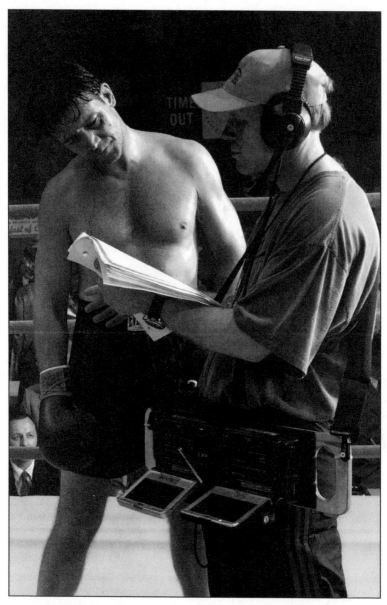

Russell Crowe and Ron Howard review a scene.

The Cinderella Story of James Braddock
A Brief History

The Jazz Age of the 1920s was a golden time for America, as the nation celebrated peace and booming prosperity on the heels of World War I. It was also a Golden Era for boxing, the brutal yet beautifully balletic sport that had captured the public imagination with its raw, primal struggles for transcendence in the ring. In the melting pot society of the early twentieth century, disparate immigrant groups drew pride from their "native" sons who boxed; communities with strong Old World roots found a focus, an expression of their heritage, each time a fighter wearing their national colors or symbol climbed into the ring.

It was during this era that James J. Braddock, a North Bergen, New Jersey-based amateur born in New York City, known for his fierce right hand, turned pro. Like many working-class kids, Braddock saw boxing as his ticket to a decent life. It was the only thing he was ever good at—and for a while he was very, very good.

His career shone with promise in the early years, when he was dubbed "the Bulldog of Bergen" for an unflinching tenacity that seemed to carry him through fights with far larger opponents. But, after sustaining irreparable damage to his badly broken right hand, his career began to slide downhill. In 1929, at the age of twenty-three, he suffered a crushing defeat at the hands of light heavyweight champ Tommy Loughran, who beat him in a fifteen-round decision that touched off a seemingly endless string of bad luck and ugly losses. Braddock was never the same again.

Nor was the nation. That same year, the stock market crashed, wiping out 40 percent of the paper values of common stock. As the shockwave spread, American families from all walks of life and every economic class lost their savings, their businesses, their homes and their farms. By 1932, nearly one in four Americans was unemployed.

The nation was reeling in shock, as throngs of once-working families began showing up at Salvation Army shelters. Food lines, work lines, and Public Relief lines—something many Americans never thought they would see in their own country—became a commonplace sight. The poorest of the poor were forced to live in "Hoovervilles," grim cardboard-shack shanty-towns that sprung up on the edges of most major cities (named with bitter irony for U.S. President Herbert Hoover, who, prior to losing the 1932 election to Franklin Delano Roosevelt, had failed to put into place any federal aid programs for struggling families). Thousands upon thousands of others roamed the country, searching for any job no matter how hard, demeaning, or dangerous. For the first time since the nation's pilgrim beginnings, many Americans faced the very real and haunting prospect of hunger and malnutrition. Suicide rates among men who had lost their jobs soared.

Like so many bankers, butchers, farmers, and factory workers, Jim Braddock watched as his life, too, began to fall apart. When the local boxing commission forced him to retire by revoking his license because of his injured right hand, Braddock searched valiantly for any available jobs, but there weren't many. He took hard-labor jobs in the shipyards, hauling sacks, or anything else he could get. Yet he was making so little that at one point, Braddock was trying to feed a family of five on just $24 a month. It seemed like a losing battle. When the family could no longer afford the basics—milk, gas, electricity—Braddock applied for Relief. It was a terrible blow to his pride, a secret shame that many who had always worked for their families were experiencing across the country.

But then in 1934, just as Roosevelt's New Deal began to kick into high gear, as Federal programs were pushed through Congress to provide relief, create jobs, and stimulate economic recovery, Braddock's luck began to shift as well. Unexpectedly, on June 14, he was given the chance to fight John "Corn" Griffin in a bout Braddock was, by all accounts, pretty much guaranteed to lose.

Instead, he managed to dance and jab his way to a win no one could quite believe—thanks in part to a newly strengthened left hand as a result of working on the docks. Braddock's share of the purse was $125. Five months later, on November 16, as if to prove it wasn't a fluke, he won a ten-round decision against Hall of Fame light heavyweight John Henry Lewis. Then, on March 22, 1935 he took on Art Lasky, who had won all but one of his last fifteen fights— yet Braddock dispatched him too in a thrilling fifteen-rounder.

With these remarkable wins, Braddock's spirit became renewed. Remarkably, one of the first things he did with his earnings was to pay back his Public Relief debt to the government. This selfless act of honor earned Braddock a new moniker among his growing ranks of American fans: "Gentleman Jim." Suddenly, with his fame beyond the boxing world increasing every day, he found himself in the unlikely position of being able to make a title shot against heavyweight champion Max Baer.

It might seem like a chance any boxer would jump at—but Braddock had plenty of reasons not to take the fight. In fact, many in the sports world warned that it was a potentially deadly match-up. Braddock was much smaller than Baer, far less experienced, and had to rely mainly on his newfound left hook, favoring his formerly injured right hand. Baer, on the other hand, had recently been brought up on manslaughter charges when one of his opponents was instantly killed by his powerhouse knockout punch. Though he was later cleared of the charges, there was little doubt that Baer, when riled up, was one of the most dangerous fighters in the sport. (Baer had also subjected opponent Ernie Schaaf to a knockout punch in the tenth round of their 1932 fight, leaving him unconscious; Schaaf later died following a bout with Primo Carnera and his death was attributed in part to the brutal beating at the hands of Baer.) In 1933, Baer fought one of the greatest matches of all time, knocking out Max Schmeling in a ten-round fight that would go down in history. In 1934, the same night that Jim Braddock fought Corn Griffin, he defeated Primo Carnera, knocking him down eleven times in eleven rounds.

Despite critics' cries that Braddock-Baer would be an unfair bout and his wife Mae's concerns that she could lose her husband to a boxing match, Braddock persevered and jumped into some of the most challenging training a boxer has ever undertaken. The build-up to the match only increased the tension, with Max Baer publicly predicting an easy knockout and reportedly taunting Braddock by calling him a "bum"—an insult Braddock definitely could not let pass without an answer.

At last, the Braddock-Baer fight took place on June 13, 1935, in front of a packed crowd of 30,000 fans in Madison Square Garden Bowl, in Long Island City, New York. Millions more huddled around their radios to hear the blow-by-blow commentary. Baer came on strong in the first few rounds, but Braddock was undeterred—fueled as he was, fighting for his family's survival. Each time one fighter dominated the round, the crowds anticipated an early end to the fight—yet the opponent invariably rallied back. This nearly impossible to call, give-and-take battle continued for an unbelievable fifteen rounds. Braddock, possessed by an unfailing spirit and pounding away with remarkable endurance, lasted all fifteen…and finally won the fight in a unanimous decision.

Instantly, it was proclaimed the greatest upset in boxing history…if not all of sports. In bars and living rooms around the country, ordinary people celebrated Braddock's championship as if he were one of their own family. The fight seemed to remind a desperate world that sometimes the down-and-out not only manage to stay alive but, in the process, become the greatest on earth. It was incredibly fitting that sportswriter Damon Runyon had dubbed Braddock the "Cinderella Man" because his rags-to-riches story so resembled a classic fairy tale. [See Runyon's foreword to a 1936 biography of Jim Braddock on opposite page.]

Braddock continued to fight, losing the heavyweight title to Joe Louis in 1937 in an eighth-round knockout (Louis was then twenty-three while Braddock was a comparatively ancient thirty-two—and Louis would later say that Braddock was one of the most courageous fighters he ever fought). He went on to beat the odds one last time, defeating the talented Tommy Farr in 1938, putting him in position to fight for the title again. But instead, he retired, saying to reporters that he was doing so not because he was done fighting but out of fairness to his wife and family.

Over the years, Braddock continued to be a hero to all those who knew his story. He was inducted into the Ring Boxing Hall of Fame in 1964 and International Boxing Hall of Fame in 2001. He served honorably in World War II and went on to own and operate heavy equipment on the same docks where he labored for a pittance during the Depression. In the 1950s, he helped to build Brooklyn's famous Verrazano Bridge, which was at the time the largest suspension bridge in the world. He died in 1974 at the age of 68.

From the Foreword
by Damon Runyon

to *Relief to Royalty: The Story of James J. Braddock*, by LUD (Ludwig Shabazian), 1936

I n all the history of the boxing game you find no human interest story to compare with the life narrative of James J. Braddock, heavyweight champion of the world.

Before Braddock came along, if any writer had offered, in fiction form, to any magazine, or to the scenario departments of the movies, the set of circumstances that befell Braddock, the tale would have been dismissed as wholly improbable.

Fiction and movie editors like their stories to be about something that could happen. This couldn't have happened—before Braddock came along. I don't want to sound trite, but believe an

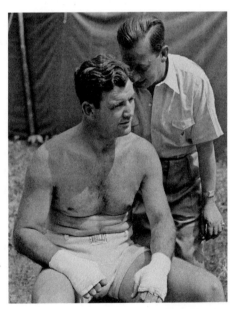

Jim Braddock and manager Joe Gould

old plot-maker, truth in Braddock's case is much stranger than fiction....

I remember Braddock as a mere stripling fighting preliminaries, with [Joe Gould, Jim's voluble manager] hanging onto the lapel of every sports writer he could catch, babbling of Braddock's future. That was around the mid-Twenties, and as the Twenties faded into the Thirties, Braddock's future seemed to be going with them.

By 1933, he was regarded as "washed up," and he vanished completely from the pugilistic news of the day. You heard rumors that he was working as a laborer on the docks over in New Jersey, then that he was on public relief, for Jim had a wife and children, and he couldn't let them starve.

You didn't see much of Joe Gould in those days, but when you did, and you asked him about Braddock, he invariably said that Jim was all right, and that he'd be back some day, and he always said it with a courage that quelled any possible doubt in your mind as to Joe's sincerity. But you didn't believe it—that Braddock was ever coming back.

Then in June of 1934, Braddock was offered a couple of hundred dollars to fight one Corn Griffin, an ex-soldier from Georgia, and it is my conjecture that Jim was expected to be a stepping stone in the advancement of Corn. It was a preliminary to the Baer-Carnera title fight, and the circumstance of Braddock getting off the floor to knock out Griffin passed almost unnoticed in the excitement of the main event.

But that night hope was born anew in Braddock's heart.

He always could punch. He found he hadn't lost his punch. He realized that he still could fight, and he felt that his Destiny, lost for many weary months, had finally found its way back to him.

The night he won the title by defeating the garrulous, flashy Max Baer, I referred to Braddock as "The Cinderella Man," for truly, here in real life, was the old story re-enacted in its elementals with a big pugilist in the leading role.

I happened to be one of the few who contend from the beginning that Braddock was entitled to the match with the champion, and after the match was made, insisted that Jim had a chance to win.

But I confess now that the night of the fight, in the face of the overwhelming public opinion against Braddock's chances, and the betting odds of 1 to 10 in favor of Baer, I commenced to weaken on my own judgment....

Only little Joe Gould, again, seemed cock-sure and confident as he stood proudly beside big Jim—that is, only Joe and Braddock. They had come a long way over a rough road together to this night.

And so Braddock won the big title, and in the time he has held it, he has endeared himself to the American pugilistic public by his unchanging modesty, his affability, and his sturdy character. His devotion to his wife and family, his capacity for "mixing," and withal his attitude as champion of the world that he will fight anybody regardless of color, or creed, has made him the most popular champion in the history of the game.

The historical pieces that follow include extracts from *The New York Times* and the *New York Post* from June 13–14, 1935, covering the Braddock-Baer fight; an interview with James Braddock from September 9, 1972; his *New York Times* obituary from November 30, 1974; and Braddock's complete fight record.

Confident Jim Braddock at Stillman's Gymasium in New York preparing for his fight with Max Baer, June 10, 1935

From *The New York Times,* June 13, 1935

KNOCKOUT VICTORY
PREDICTED BY BAER

Max, Expressing Respect for Foe's Hitting Power, Hopes to End Battle Early.

BRADDOCK IS CONFIDENT

Declares He Will Force the Fighting in Every Round and Capture Title.

Statements regarding plans of action for tonight's heavyweight championship fight were given to *The New York Times* yesterday by the principals, Max Baer and James J. Braddock, and their respective managers, Ancil Hoffman and Joe Gould. The statements follow:

BAER—I am going in there to put Braddock away as quickly as I can. Don't get me wrong, I don't regard Jimmy as an easy opponent. But he's a hitter, and hitters are dangerous. I intend to come out of my corner slashing at him, and I hope to put him down early. I know Braddock can hit, and I think that he will stand back and wait to reach me with his right hand. But I don't intend to let him do that. My plan is to go at him and send all I can at him. Remember, I'm in swell shape, and if I don't get Braddock in the first round, it won't take me very long after that.

HOFFMAN—It seems to me that Baer should win by a knockout in ten rounds, at the most. He'll go after Braddock and try to finish him as quickly as he can, of course, but if he fails to stop the challenger in the early rounds, he'll wait for his second wind. He can go the fifteen rounds very easily, and when the tenth or eleventh round comes along, he'll be just as strong as when the fight started, and that's when he'll finish Braddock. Make no mistake about it, Max is in the best condition of his career, and he will be able to stand up all night long against Braddock's body punching.

BRADDOCK—I am going into this fight confident that I will win.

James Braddock and Max Baer, June 13, 1935

I have no fear of Baer. I know how he fights and I intend to make him fight every minute he is in there. He'll get no rest. I will knock him out if I can and I am sure I can outbox him. I am in fine condition and am a better fighter than I have ever been. I am heavier and stronger and even faster than when I weighed less. I am used to having the odds against me, but I don't pay much attention to odds. When it is over I will be the new champion of the world.

GOULD—In spite of the opinion of most of the experts in the country, I feel certain Braddock will win the world heavyweight title. It's in the air. He is in condition, and that is the main thing. I regard it as a good omen that the odds are against us. We are used to it, and the bigger the better. The favorites against Jimmy have always wound up losers. Jimmy will surprise a lot of people tonight.

From *The New York Times*, June 14, 1935

Braddock Outpoints Baer to Win World Ring Title

New Jersey Heavyweight, on Relief Within Last Two Years, Caps Great Come-Back by Victory in Bowl—Takes 9 to 15 Rounds.

By James P. Dawson

The wholly unexpected happened last night under a hazy moon in the Madison Square Garden Bowl, which spreads over Long Island City's acres.

James J. Braddock, born on New York's West Side, but now a resident of New Jersey, won the world's heavyweight championship from Max Baer, the playboy of the ring, who could not be serious even while a fortune was slipping through his fingers.

In fifteen rounds of fighting that was surprisingly easy for him as it started, but grew more painful and more grueling, Braddock, man of destiny, who was regarded as a has-been no longer ago than the Fall of 1933, scaled the ring's heights on his lion-hearted courage and a grim determination.

He hammered his way to the decision over Baer to the complete satisfaction of some 30,000 wild-eyed fight fans who paid estimated gross receipts of $200,000....

Referee Johnny McAvoy and the two judges, Charley Lynch and George Kelly, voted unanimously for Braddock as the new champion without a dissenting voice from the throng. It was impossible to obtain a round-by-round detail of the officials' vote, but none was necessary.

Hardly a critic at the ringside disagreed with the award. Certainly none in the crowd, not even the enthusiastic friends of the playboy, who is now an ex-champion, could disagree.

There was no room for doubt because Braddock won by nine rounds to six. That is the writer's score, and it is also the general score of critics who viewed the battle from their close-up chairs in the glare of the ring's strong lights....

From *The New York Times*, June 14, 1935

Mrs. Braddock Weeps Happily on Hearing Decision Over Radio

But She Refuses to Wake Her Three Children to Whom New Champion Had Promised He Would 'Bring Home the Bacon'— Laughter and Gayety Echo in New Jersey Home After Fight.

Tears of happiness and relief streamed down the face of Mrs. James J. Braddock last night as the radio in the home of her parents at 50 Twenty-fifty Street, Guttenberg, N.J., conveyed the news that she was the wife of the new heavyweight champion of the world, the man whom all the experts said would be beaten by Max Baer.

Her mother, Mrs. Peter Fox, squeezed Mrs. Braddock's hand and there were tears in the older eyes, too, while photographers took pictures of the two women and newspapermen clustered around with questions.

In a near-by room slept the Braddocks' three small children. Mrs. Braddock would not wake them last night to tell them the news. They are James Jay, 4½; Howard, a year younger; and Rose Marie, just past two.

Shows Fine Control

The young matron, who said she would never watch her husband fight again, having left in the middle of one of his battles just after they were married six years ago, stood the ordeal, for it was one for her, last night with admirable control.

As the minutes crept toward the time when the fight in the Madison Square Garden Bowl in Long Island City was to begin, her face became strained and she moved restlessly in her chair, which flanked the cabinet radio. Reporters and photographers climbed the stairs to the apartment on the third floor of the three-family house. Her father entertained the newspapermen with beer in the kitchen during the battle.

Her nervousness increased as the fight began and the radio car-

ried the story of its progress. Her hands alternately relaxed and clenched as Braddock either gained a point or was hammered by Baer. But there were no tears, even though the eyes were veiled and cast toward the floor during almost the entire fifteen rounds.

Jim Braddock's wife Mae and children James, Rose Marie, and Howard

Excitement and Happiness

The moments of suspense, waiting for the decision after the fifteenth round had ended, were perhaps the worst. The radio blared:

"There is a new ★ ★ ★"

The room did not wait for the announcer to finish. Those present burst into happy excited exclamation and laughter.

For a second or two, no one thought of Mrs. Braddock. The significance of the decision held all thought on the Long Island City arena. Then they turned toward Mrs. Braddock, to find tears rolling down her cheeks. But she was smiling and laughing softly, while her mother, also crying, held her daughter's hand and patted it.

"It took a lot to hold it in," Mrs. Braddock said.

She listened eagerly as her husband was brought to the microphone and his voice came over the air.

"What were you thinking about during the fight?"

"I was thinking of the wife and kids," came Braddock's reply. "I told them that I was going to bring home the bacon and I knew I had to make the grade."

Mrs. Braddock smiled to herself.

"What are you going to do tomorrow?" the new champion was asked.

"I'm going home to see the wife and kiddies," and then as an afterthought, "and I'm going to collect the dough."

The tension was relieved and Mrs. Braddock laughed heartily, all her fear and apprehension gone.

From *New York Post*, June 14, 1935

Baer's Hands Broken, Two Doctors Declare

Compound Fracture in Right, Simple in Left, Say Physicians After Examination—Through, Max Insists

Two physicians examined Max Baer's hands today and announced that both of them were broken.

The celebrated Baer right that failed to put away James J. Braddock last night had a compound fracture, they said, and the left a simple fracture.

But a third physician who X-rayed the hands said, according to Baer, that his first examination showed only a chipped bone in the left hand and an old fracture of the right.

"Boys, don't pay any attention to my hands," said Baer to newspapermen....."They'll say, 'He lost and he's trying to alibi. Carnera did that with his ankle.'

"No alibis—the better man won."

Braddock's Comment

The comment of the better man James J. Braddock was:

"So he signs a thousand autographs after the fight and now he says his hands are broken."

Baer did not seem worried about the loss of the championship. He announced that he did not intend to fight again, that he had plenty of money put away and that he is going to raise cattle, act in the movies and broadcast....

Braddock meanwhile was being initiated in the clamor and attention that surrounds a champion. He took it as phlegmatically as he took the many reverses in the ring which preceded his amazing rise from the relief rolls to the heavyweight championship.

He spent the day surrounded by newspapermen, photographs and newsreel men, posing with his wife, telling about the fight, referring inquiries about his fistic future to his happy and excited manager, Joe Gould.

Telegrams poured in on him. Mae West asked for his photograph. He got an offer from Walter Rothenburg, the German promoter who is so generous with his offers, for a match with Max Schmeling in Amsterdam for $100,000.

And just a year ago he was glad to take $250 for beating Corn Griffin and starting his march from a has-been to champion. He remained the calmest of the many persons around him.

"In His Own Words,"
by James J. Braddock

Interviewed on September 9, 1972,
from *In This Corner*, by Peter Heller, DaCapo Press, 1994

Damon Runyon was the guy that give me the name "The Cinderella Man." That's on account of in '32 and '33 and part of '34 I was more or less forgotten in boxing. Then I made the comeback and knocked out John Henry Lewis. I was on welfare. That was in '32, '33. I didn't fight that much and I was working on the docks. I had three kids and a wife I had to support. The family was growing up and I was making enough money to support them, the food on the table, and have a home, but things were a little rough. I guess with everybody at that time you'd find spots where you need a little cash that you didn't have. That was in the town [North Bergen, New Jersey] right here. They paid me. I returned it; let them give it to somebody else because they were good enough to give it to me. [I was in] a spot where I could pay it back. He picked up the story, Damon Runyon, the way things were and then I come back to win the heavyweight title. I was a pauper and then I was a prince, so he gave me the name of "The Cinderella Man" of boxing.

It was one of them things that happens in life to people. You're not always in the right spot at the right time, and that happened to me. I was licked quite a few times. I lost about 21 fights all together out of 80-some-odd. That's boxing. You get the breaks and you don't get the breaks. If you get the breaks you're in there, you're up on the top, but if you don't you're on the bottom. I was more or less always the underdog. It didn't make no difference to me. Corn Griffin, that was in '34, I knocked him out on the Baer-Carnera card when Baer won the title. He had me on the deck. He hit me with a right hand behind the ear. He was a left hooker and I always had a lot of success with left hookers. I had a fast right hand and coming in with a left hook you meet a guy with a right hand and if you hit him in the right spot, which I done to him, I hit him right on the chin and that was it. He was boxing with Carnera in the camp and, according to the reporters, he was licking Carnera every day they boxed. He was rated a pretty good fighter at that time. Not only that fight, but in the next one, knocking out a guy that had previously outpointed me, John Henry Lewis, and then coming on in March the next year to beat Art Lasky, who was the number one contender, that pushed me right into the position of being the number one contender for Max's title. Steve Hamas and Art Lasky, they were the two leading contenders, and they fought and Lasky outpointed Steve. Steve then went to Germany to box Max Schmeling, who he had previously licked, and Steve was knocked out by Schmeling in Germany. So they matched Lasky and I. There was no talk about a heavyweight championship fight because they figured Lasky'd lick me. When I beat him in 15 rounds I hit him with everything. I mean, wherever his kisser was, I had a punch there, a left hook, a right cross, it was just one of them nights. It was one of my good fights. I beat Art in 15 rounds in Madison Square Garden, which was in April of '34. Then in June when I boxed Max Baer for the title, which was three months later, I started to put some weight on, about 10 pounds, which I needed, and I had no trouble beating Baer.

They gave me the shot at the title and then I went on to box Baer and beat him. They might have been figuring that I was a tune-up for a Louis fight. The idea was when you got in there to fight, when the bell rings you're in there to win, and if your ability matches the other guy's and it's a little better than his, then you win the fight. If it doesn't it's to his advantage. That's the way I always looked at it. Any time I was to fight anybody, he didn't mean one thing to me, I mean about being scared of somebody. It was all an even thing in that respect. I thought I could lick Baer. I thought I can outpoint him. They never gave the advantage that I had a chance. But my punching ability had a lot to do with it, too. I could punch pretty good. He was just another opponent and I was in there to fight him. I know what I got and I'm going to use it. If it's good enough to lick him, that's it. I knew from the start that I could lick him. I seen Tommy Loughran lick him in the Garden, see, and I boxed Tommy and I knew what kind of a boxer he was and I said to myself, this was '29 or '30, this was five years before I boxed him, I said to myself if I ever fought Baer I'd do the same Loughran done with him, the left hand and move, which I done the night of the fight. That was on my mind all the time. I hit him with a couple of good right hands of my own. Oh, yeah, he landed. Dynamite puncher. If he hit you right, he'd knock you out in the third row. In my opinion, the guy was a harder puncher than Louis. Louis was a faster puncher and he hit you more punches, but Baer was a guy that could hurt you. He hit me a couple of times and I said, "Is that as hard as you can punch?" So that took a little bit out of him. I said to him, around the eighth round, I said, "Hey, Max, you better get going. You're way behind." I kept sticking him.

You see, Max, he was a nice fellow but he never should have been a fighter. His ability was, if the guy could have got mad, you know, like guys get in a fight, he'd kill you with a punch, because he had killed a couple of guys, and I think that was on his mind. But I always said that Max should have been an actor instead of a fighter.

Right from the eighth or ninth round I knew it, because he wasn't getting any better and I was doing a little better. I was reaching him with more jabs. I remember it was tougher getting back to the dressing room that night than it ever was before. They were pulling my hair, they were reaching over, I had bodyguards taking me through, they were reaching over just to touch me, to let you know they were there. It was a great night, and we got a lot of nice accolades from different people around the country.

The New York Times, November 30, 1974

Braddock, Who Beat Baer for Title, Dies

North Bergen, NJ, Nov. 29 (AP)—James J. Braddock, who won the world heavyweight championship in 1935 by outpointing Max Baer in one of boxing's biggest upsets, died today at his home here. He was 68 years old.

Surviving are his widow, the former Mae Fox; two sons, Howard and Jay; a daughter, Rose Marie DeWitt; four brothers, two sisters, and six grandchildren.

Diffident Demeanor
By Joe Nichols

Jimmy Braddock of the soft voice, twisted smile and diffident demeanor looked more like the old-time friendly Irish cop on the beat than a prize fighter. His patient manner marked his everyday pose just as it did his way of going into the ring. To those who knew him well the nickname Plain Jim, handed to him by John Kieran was far more descriptive than the more famous sobriquet of Cinderella Man that Damon Runyon dubbed him.

And yet, there was pertinence in Runyon's name for Braddock. The fighter's professional career was a true sign of the ring, embracing as it did a promising start, a skid to oblivion and retirement, a desperate return to fighting from the relief rolls of the Depression era and, as a fairy tale climax, the winning of the heavyweight boxing championship of the world, the richest individual prize in the realm of sports.

This final achievement was as surprising in its way as the miraculous climb of the 1969 Mets in baseball greatness. For Braddock had to hurdle three heavily favored and highly rated foes at the time to get the shot at the title. And to get the title he had to fight and beat Max Baer, a mighty hitter whose strength and awesome reputation made him the favorite at odds of 10 to 1, and even more.

But on the night of June 13, 1935, in the Madison Square Garden Bowl in Long Island City, Queens, Braddock brought off the boxing miracle of the time. He boxed his way, patiently and craftily, to the unanimous decision over the baffled Baer in 15 rounds.

Again, on June 22, 1937, Braddock was the short-ender in the betting in a fight with Joe Louis, but this time Braddock lost his title by a knockdown in eight rounds. Before bowing to Louis, though, Braddock had the satisfaction of knocking him down in the fourth round. The Cinderella era having closed, Braddock had only one more regular fight after that, a 10-round decision conquest of Tommy Farr on January 21, 1938.

His complete ring career embraced 84 bouts with 52 victories of which 28 were knockouts, 21 defeats including two knockouts, three draws, two no contests and six no decisions. He stood 6 feet 2½ inches tall and, for his title fight with Baer, weighed 190 pounds.

Braddock was born here [New York City] on Dec. 6, 1905. When he was a child his family moved to West New York, N.J., just the other side of the Hudson River. He engaged in his first amateur bout at the age of 17, and it was not until he was 20 that he turned professional as a middleweight (160 pounds).

He built up a good record frequently beating heavier opponents, and in 1929, having reached the light heavyweight class of 175 pounds, he met Tommy Loughran in a bid for the latter's championship of that division, but was outpointed.

Went Into Decline

He went into decline after that, and lost frequently until, after breaking a hand in a fight with Abe Feldman on Sept. 25, 1933, he gave up the ring to become a longshoreman. Work was scarce in that line, and Braddock was forced to apply for relief to support his wife and three children. It is a frequently repeated story that, as soon as he became solvent again, Braddock repaid every cent of the $17 a week relief money to the agencies.

Early in 1934 a fighter named Corn Griffin from Georgia appeared on the heavyweight scene, and a local heavyweight "name" was sought to oppose him in a frank effort to build him up as a championship contender. Braddock was working on the docks, but his friend and manager, Joe Biegel, professionally known as Joe Gould, persuaded Mike Jacobs, the promoter to accept Braddock as a sacrificial lamb for Griffin. On June 14, in a preliminary to the championship fight between Baer and the unsuccessful defender, Primo Carnera, Braddock knocked the favored Griffin out in three rounds.

After that surprise victory, Braddock successively defeated John Henry Lewis and Art Lasky, and earned the match with Baer. That triumph brought financial security to Braddock, according to the custom of the era, profited through personal appearances and testimonials for two years before risking his title. It was in his first defense, against Joe Louis, in Chicago, that Braddock was dethroned by a knockout in eight rounds.

James J. Braddock, circa 1938

JAMES J. BRADDOCK'S FIGHT RECORD

Key: W: Won decision; KO: Won by knockout; TK: Won by technical knockout; L: Lost; LT: Lost by technical knockout; LK: Lost by
knockout; LD: Lost decision; LF: Lost on foul; NC: No contest;
DR: Draw; ND: No decision; EXH: Exhibition; CANC: Canceled

Date	Opponent	Place	Result	
1926				
Apr. 14	Al Settle	West Hoboken, NJ	ND	4
Apr. 22	George Deschner	Ridgefield Park, NJ	KO	2
May	Phil Weisberger	Jersey City, NJ	KO	1
May	Jack O'Day	Jersey City, NJ	KO	1
May	Willie Daily	Jersey City, NJ	KO	1
June 18	Leo Dobson	Jersey City, NJ	KO	1
June 28	Jim Pearson	Jersey City, NJ	KO	2
July 9	Walter Westman	Jersey City, NJ	TK	3
Sept. 7	Gene Travers	Jersey City, NJ	KO	1
Sept. 13	Mike Rock	Jersey City, NJ	KO	1
Sept. 16	Ray Kennedy	West New York, NJ	KO	1
Sept. 30	Carmine Caggiano	West New York, NJ	KO	1
Nov. 12	Lou Barba	New York, NY	W	6
Dec. 4	Al Settle	New York, NY	W	6
Dec. 8	Joe Hudson	New York, NY	W	6
Dec. 20	Norman Conrad	Jersey City, NJ	ND	4
1927				
Jan. 28	George Larocco	New York, NY	KO	1
Feb. 1	Johnny Alberts	Wilkes-Barre, PA	KO	4
Feb. 15	Jack Nelson	Wilkes-Barre, PA	W	6
Mar.	Tom McKiernan	–	KO	2
Mar. 3	Lou Barba	New York, NY	W	4
Mar. 8	Nick Fadil	New York, NY	W	6
Apr. 19	Frankie Lennon	Wilkes-Barre, PA	KO	3
May 2	Stanley Simmons	Jersey City, NJ	TK	1
May 11	Jack Stone	West New York, NJ	ND	10
May 20	George Larocco	New York, NY	DR	6
May 27	Paul Cavalier	Rochelle Park, NJ	ND	10
June 8	Jimmy Francis	West New York, NJ	ND	10
July 13	Jimmy Francis	Union City, NJ	ND	10
July 21	George Larocco	New York, NY	W	6

Aug. 10	Vic McLaughlin	West New York, NJ	ND	10
Sept. 21	Herman Heller	West New York, NJ	ND	10
Oct. 5	Joe Monte	New York, NY	DR	10

1928

Jan. 6	Paul Swiderski	New York, NY	W	8
May 7	Jack Darnell	Jersey City, NJ	KO	4
May 16	Jimmy Francis	West New York, NJ	ND	10
June 7	Joe Monte	New York, NY	L	10
June 27	Billy Vidabeck	West New York, NJ	ND	10
July 25	Nando Tassi	New York, NY	DR	10
Aug. 8	Joe Sekyra	New York, NY	L	10
Oct. 17	Pete Latzo	Newark, NJ	W	10
Nov. 30	Gerald Griffith	New York, NY	KO	2

1929

Jan. 18	Leo Lomski	New York, NY	L	10
Feb. 4	George Gemas	Newark, NJ	KO	1
Mar. 11	Jimmy Slattery	New York, NY	TK	9
Apr. 22	Eddie Benson	Buffalo, NY	KO	1
July 18	Tommy Loughran	New York, NY	L	15
Aug. 27	Yale Okun	Los Angeles, CA	L	10
Nov. 15	Maxie Rosenbloom	New York, NY	L	10
Dec. 7	Jack Warren	Brooklyn, NY	KO	2

1930

Jan. 17	Leo Lomski	Chicago, IL	L	10
Apr. 7	Billy Jones	Philadelphia, PA	L	10
June 5	Harold Mays	West New York, NJ	ND	10
July 2	Joe Monte	Boston, MA	W	10
Aug. 11	Alvin Hunt	Boston, MA	L	10
Sept. 19	Phil Mercurio	Boston, MA	KO	2

1931

Jan. 23	Ernie Schaaf	New York, NY	L	10
Mar. 5	Jack Roper	Miami, FL	KO	1
Mar. 30	Jack Kelly	New Haven, CT	W	10
Sept. 3	Andy Mitchell	Detroit, MI	DR	10
Oct. 9	Joe Sekyra	New York, NY	L	10
Nov. 10	Maxie Rosenbloom	Minneapolis, MN	NC	2
Dec. 4	Al Gainer	New Haven, CT	L	10

1932

| Mar. 18 | Baxter Calmes | Chicago, IL | L | 10 |

May 13	Charley Retzlaff	Boston, MA	L	10
June 21	Vincent Parille	New York, NY	W	5
July 25	Tony Shucco	New York, NY	L	8
Sept. 21	John Henry Lewis	San Francisco, CA	L	10
Sept. 30	Dynamite Jackson	San Diego, CA	W	10
Oct. 21	Tom Patrick	Hollywood, CA	L	10
Nov. 9	Lou Scozza	San Francisco, CA	LT	6

1933

Jan. 13	Martin Levandowski	Chicago, IL	W	10
Jan. 20	Hans Birkie	New York, NY	L	10
Mar. 1	Al Ettore	Philadelphia, PA	LF	4
Mar. 21	Al Stillman	St. Louis, MO	TK	10
Apr. 5	Martin Levandowski	St. Louis, MO	L	10
May 19	Al Stillman	St. Louis, MO	L	10
June 21	Les Kennedy	Jersey City, NJ	W	10
July 21	Chester Matan	West New York, NJ	W	10
Sept. 25	Abe Feldman	Mount Vernon, NY	NC	6

1934

| June 14 | John Griffin | Long Island City, NY | TK | 3 |
| Nov. 16 | John Henry Lewis | New York, NY | W | 10 |

1935

| Mar. 22 | Art Lasky | New York, NY | W | 15 |
| June 13 | Max Baer | Long Island City, NY | W | 15 |

Becomes the Heavyweight Champion of the World

July 18	Jack McCarthy	Columbus, OH	EXH	3
Aug. 27	Jack McCarthy	Houston, TX	EXH	3
Nov. 5	Jack McCarthy	Seattle, WA	EXH	3
Nov. 12	Jack McCarthy	Portland, OR	EXH	2
Nov. 15	Jack McCarthy	San Francisco, CA	EXH	3
Nov. 20	Jack McCarthy	Oakland, CA	EXH	3

1936

| Sept. 30 | Max Schmeling | New York, NY | CANC | |

1937

| June 22 | Joe Louis | Chicago, IL | LK | 8 |

1938

| Jan. 21 | Tommy Farr | New York, NY | W | 10 |

1941

| Mar. 26 | Clarence Burman | Charlotte, NC | EXH | 5 |

CAST AND CREW CREDITS

UNIVERSAL PICTURES, MIRAMAX FILMS and IMAGINE ENTERTAINMENT
Present
A BRIAN GRAZER Production
In Association with PARKWAY PRODUCTIONS
A RON HOWARD Film

RUSSELL CROWE   RENÉE ZELLWEGER

CINDERELLA MAN

PAUL GIAMATTI   CRAIG BIERKO   PADDY CONSIDINE
BRUCE MCGILL   RON CANADA   NICHOLAS CAMPBELL
ROSEMARIE DEWITT   RANCE HOWARD   CLINT HOWARD
CONNOR PRICE   ARIEL WALLER   PATRICK LOUIS
ANGELO DUNDEE   CHUCK SHAMATA

Directed by
RON HOWARD

Executive Producer
TODD HALLOWELL

Music by
THOMAS NEWMAN

Screenplay by
CLIFF HOLLINGSWORTH
and AKIVA GOLDSMAN

Director of Photography
SALVATORE TOTIN

Production Designer
WYNN THOMAS

Casting by
JANE JENKINS, C.S.A
JANET HIRSHENSON, C.S.A

Story by
CLIFF HOLLINGSWORTH

Edited by
MIKE HILL, A.C.E.
DAN HANLEY, A.C.E

Co-Executive Producer
JAMES WHITAKER

Produced by
BRIAN GRAZER
RON HOWARD
PENNY MARSHALL

Costume Designer
DANIEL ORLANDI

Associate Producers
LOUISA VELIS
KATHLEEN McGILL

CAST

Jim Braddock . . . . RUSSELL CROWE
Mae Braddock . . . . RENÉE ZELLWEGER
Joe Gould . . . . PAUL GIAMATTI
Max Baer . . . . CRAIG BIERKO
Mike Wilson . . . . PADDY CONSIDINE
Jimmy Johnston . . . . BRUCE McGILL
Ford Bond . . . . DAVID HUBAND
Jay Braddock . . . . CONNOR PRICE
Rosemarie Braddock . . . . ARIEL WALLER
Howard Braddock . . . . PATRICK LOUIS
Sara . . . . ROSEMARIE DeWITT
Lucille Gould . . . . LINDA KASH
Sporty Lewis . . . . NICHOLAS CAMPBELL
Jake . . . . GENE PYRZ
Father Rorick . . . . CHUCK SHAMATA
Joe Jeanette . . . . RON CANADA

Alice . . . . ALICIA JOHNSTON
John Henry Lewis . . . . TROY AMOS-ROSS
Art Lasky . . . . MARK SIMMONS
Corn Griffin . . . . ART BINKOWSKI
Abe Feldman . . . . DAVID LITZINGER
Primo Carnera . . . . MATTHEW G. TAYLOR
Announcer Al Fazin . . . . RANCE HOWARD
Official (Griffin/Baer fight) . . . . JAMES RITZ
Referee McAvoy . . . . FULVIO CECERE
Referees . . . . CLINT HOWARD
GERRY ELLISON
BILL MACKIE
RAY MARSH
FERNAND CHRETIEN
DAVE DUNBAR
Ancil Hoffman . . . . KEN JAMES
Lewis Coach . . . . RUFUS CRAWFORD

Angelo the Cornerman . . . . ANGELO DUNDEE
Braddock Cornermen . . . . LOU EISEN
                      WAYNE GORDON
Baer Cornermen . . . . WAYNE FLEMMING
                      NICK ALACHIOTIS
Lewis Cornermen . . . . . . CHRISTOPHER D. AMOS
                      NICK CARUSI
Lasky Cornermen . . . . KEITH MURPHY
                      EVERTON MCEWAN
                      JOHNNY KALBHENN
Griffin Cornermen . . . . DAVID GEORGIEFF
                      WAYNE BOURQUE
                      PAUL RYAN
Feldman Cornermen . . . . SEAN GILROY
                      MICHAEL MCNAMARA
Carnera Cornermen . . . . BILLY WINE
                      RICHARD SUTTON
                      MICHAEL CHIN
Campbell Cornermen . . . . STEWART LUNN
                      RICHARD LEWIS
                      PETER WYLIE
Tuffy Griffith . . . . THOMASZ KURZYDLOWSKI
Frankie Campbell . . . . STUART CLARK
Undercard Boxers (Feldman) . . . NICK ALACHIOTIS
                      JULIAN LEWIS
Announcer (Lasky) . . . . ERIC FINK
Young Reporter . . . . SERGIO DI ZIO
Reporters . . . . GAVIN GRAZER
                      BOYD BANKS
                      DANIEL KASH
                      JUDAH KATZ
                      ANGELO TSAROUCHAS
                      ROBERT SMITH
1928 Fans . . . . CRAIG WARNOCK
                      AARON ABRAMS
1935 Fans . . . . DUFF MACDONALD
                      ANDREW STELMACK
                      CHRIS CRUMB
Quincy . . . . GERRY QUIGLEY
Electric Man . . . . PETER MACNEILL
Promoter . . . . DARRIN BROWN
Dock Workers . . . . JOHN HEALY
                      PETER DIDIANO
                      JAMES KIRCHNER
                      MIKE LANGLOIS
Angry Woman . . . . MAGDALENA ALEXANDER
Relief Office Woman . . . . NOLA AUGUSTSON
Waiter . . . . GINO MARROCCO
George . . . . MARK TAYLOR
Lady . . . . SHARRON MATTHEWS
Church Man . . . . ALEC STOCKWELL
Church Old Man . . . . CHICK ROBERTS
Church Girl . . . . ISABELLA FINK
Sam . . . . BEAU STARR

Radio Commentator . . . . PHILIP CRAIG
Hooverville Cops . . . . ROMAN PODHORA
                      R.D. REID
Hooverville Man . . . . MICHAEL DYSON
Gibson . . . . SAM MALKIN
Sam Penny . . . . TONY MUNCH
Limo Driver . . . . CONRAD BERGSCHNEIDER
Announcer (Griffith) . . . . RICHARD BINSLEY
Flapper Girls . . . . RAMONA PRINGLE
                      KATRINA MATTHEWS SWAIN
Jay Braddock (4 yrs.) . . . . COOPER BRACKEN
                      JACOB BRACKEN
Deserting Father . . . . ALON NASHMAN
Junket . . . . DOMENIC CUZZOCREA
Security Guard . . . . NEIL FOSTER
Cop . . . . BRIAN JAGERSKY
Fight Promoters . . . . RAY KERR
                      TIM EDDIS
Mr. Mills . . . . DAVE ARKELL
Mother . . . . DEBRA SHERMAN
Baer Hotel Hotties . . . . JOANNE RITCEY
                      ALEX CAIRNS
Man on Street . . . . GEORGE DUFF

Boxing Choreographer . . . . NICK POWELL
Boxing/Stunt Coordinator . . . . . STEVE LUCESCU
Stunts . . . . STUART CLARK

CHRIS MCGUIRE	MARK TAYLOR
DEAN COPKOV	NICK POWELL
DAVE VAN ZEYL	ROBERT RACKI
ED QUEFFELEC	JIM LYTLE
JAMES BINKLEY	JOEL HARRIS
BRAD BENNETT	ROB MACDONALD
MARCO BIANCO	ROB BELL
RON VAN HART	DONOVAN BOUCHER
CHRIS JOHNSON	DUNCAN MCLEOD
EGGERTON MARCUS	DEXTER DELVES
TEBOR BROSCH	BILLY OLIVER
JOHN STONEHAM JR.	BRYAN RENFRO
PAUL RUTLEDGE	SHAWN ORR
RICK PARKER	PATRICK MARK
COTTON MATHER	KEVIN RUSHTON

Unit Production Manager . . . . KATHLEEN MCGILL
First Assistant Director . . . . WILLIAM M. CONNOR

Unit Production Manager . . . . . STEVE WAKEFIELD
Second Assistant Director . . . ANDREW ROBINSON
Art Directors . . . . PETER GRUNDY
                      DAN YARHI
Assistant Art Directors . . . . BRAD MILBURN
                      JOHN MORAN
                      YASSARA MONTELEONE
Graphic Designer . . . . PAUL GREENBERG

Storyboard Artist . . . . Rob Ballantyne
Art Department Coordinator . . Elizabeth Moran
Asset/Clearances/Product Placement . . . .
Andrew Rosen
Art Department Apprentices . . . . . . Dennis Nam
Paul To
Set Decorator . . . . Gordon Sim
Set Designers . . . .
Michael Madden   Gordon White
David Hirschfield   Russell Moore
Property Master . . . . Tory Bellingham
Assistant Property Master . . . . Jeff Poulis
Props Buyer . . . . . . Anne Marie Ferney-Tellez
Props Assistant . . . . Toni Wong
Lead Set Dresser . . . . Keith Sly
Leadman . . . . Carlos Caneca
Buyers . . . . Marlene Rain
Odetta Stoddard
Terry Edwards
On Set Dresser . . . . David Evans
Assistant On Set Dresser . . . . . . Robert Shipman
Set Dressers . . . .
J. Tracy Budd   Mike Franklin
Stephen Hayes   Dana Richardson
A Camera Operator . . . . Salvatore Totino
A Camera First Assistants . . . . Jesse Green
Russel Bowie
A Camera Second Assistant . . . . . Ian Anderson
Camera Loader . . . . Marzena Bielewicz
B Camera/Steadicam Operator . . . .
Candide Franklyn
B Camera First Assistant . . . . John Harper
B Camera Second Assistant . . . . . Jaclyn Young
C Camera Operator . . . . Keith Hlady
C Camera First Assistant . . . . Rich Green
C Camera Second Assistant . . . . Ari Magder
Second Loader . . . . Darcy Gasparovic
D Camera Operator . . . . Peter Luxford
D Camera First Assistant . . . . Dean Stinchcombe
E Camera Operator . . . . Mike Hall
E Camera First Assistant . . . . Mark Nener
E Camera Second Assistant . . Rachael Thompson
Third Loader . . . . Kirsta Teague
Video Assist Operator . . . . Paul Thompson
Asst. Video Assist Operator . . Anthony Nocera
Video Assistant . . . . Kelly Hearns
Production Sound Mixer . . . . . John J. Thomson
Boom Operator . . . . Alan Zielonko
Cableman . . . . Sean Armstrong
First Assistant Editors . . . . Robert Komatsu
Irene Kassow
Second Assistant Editor . . . . Kent Blocher
Assistant Editor . . . . Guy Barresi

Assistant Editor (Toronto) . . . . . Brigitte Rabazo
Trainee Assistant Editor . . . . Luis Freitas
Technocrane Technician . . . . Rick Leger
Gaffers . . . . Jay Fortune
Bob McRae
Best Boy . . . . Douglas G. Reid
Electrics . . Don Caulfield   Duane Gullison
Marvin Macina   Larry Smith
Craig Bulmer
Rigging Gaffer . . . . John Ferguson

Rigging Best Boy . . . . Tim Lovell
Rigging Electrics . . . . Barry Goodwin
Norm O'Halloran
Dave Kellner
Generator Operator . . . . Hugh Young
Key Grip . . . . Richard Emerson
Best Boy Grip . . . . Sean Bourdeau
Dolly Grip . . . . Robert Cochrane
Grips . . . .
Keith Adams   Jeff Heintzman
Martin Lake   Robert Vigus
Key Rigging Grip . . . . Roy Elliston
Rigging Grip Best Boy . . . . . . Mongo Andrews
Rigging Grips . . . .
Tony Dubreuil   Peter Schalakowskyj
Ron Muise   Andre Ouimet
SFX Coordinator . . . . Laird McMurray
SFX Key . . . . Stani Veselinovic
SFX Rigging Key . . . . Stephen Wallace
Assistant SFX . . . . Peter Fletcher
SFX Shop Key . . . . Lisa Pacitto
SFX Technicians . . . . Brad Larkin
David Reaume
Peter Sissakis
Costume Supervisor . . . . Dan Bronson
Assistant Costume Designer . . . . . . Luis Sequeira
Costume Supervisor . . . . Lindsay Jacobs
Set Supervisor . . . . Wayne Godfrey
Dressers . . . . Michael Castellano
Christina Cattle
Assistant Costume Designer (LA) . . . .
Marjorie McCowan
Costumer . . . . Andrea Knaub
Extras Coordinator . . . . Ian Drummond
Costume Buyer . . . . Sara Schilt
Wardrobe Assistant . . . . John Girouard

Special Makeup Effects by . . . .
David Leroy Anderson

AFX STUDIOS
HEATHER LANGENKAMP ANDERSON

JOHN WHEATON	NICOLE MICHAUD
DAMON BISHOP	FRANCOIS DAGENAIS
TONY ACOSTA	CHRIS BRIDGES
	TONY LABATT

Key SFX Makeup . . . . LANCE ANDERSON
SFX Makeup Technicians . . . . SEAN SANSOM
PATRICK BAXTER

Ms. Zellweger's Makeup . . . . GRAHAM JOHNSTON
Key Makeup Artist. . . . . ANN BRODIE
Makeup Artists. . . . . DOROTA ZAJAC
BURTON LEBLANC
Key Hair Stylist. . . . . VINCENT SULLIVAN
Mr. Crowe's Hair Stylist . . . . MANNY MILLAR
Ms. Zellweger's Hair Stylist . . COLLEEN CALLAGHAN
Hair Stylists. . . . .

CAROL HARTWICK	JANICE MILLER
HAZEL GORDON	LINDA MONTGOMERIE

Script Supervisor . . . . ANNA RANE
Location Manager. . . . . KEITH LARGE
Assistant Location Managers . . ALEX MCNAUGHTON
GREG MCMASTER
PETER BIRD
Location Set P.A.s . . . .

PATRICK DAVIS	MATT GRAVER
JOHN TEIXEIRA	DAVID BLACKER
DAVID FRANKLIN	HAROLD FRANCIS
KYRA RATTRAY	MARY MILOVAC
KAITLIN JACOBS	PAUL FRANKLIN

Production Accountant . . . . . . ELAINE THURSTON
Assistant Accountant . . . . LUC BERNARD
Payroll Accountant . . . . GERRY ALFONSO
2nd Assistant Accountants. . . . . . . KEVIN ALAKAS
TRACEY PHILLIPS
3rd Assistant Accountants . . . MICHELLE BERRIGAN
DEVIN WHITE
Production Coordinator . . . . VAIR MACPHEE
Asst. Production Coordinator. . DAVID M. CHISHOLM
Production Secretary . . . . MICHELLE K. SMITH
2nd 2nd Assistant Director . . . . . DARRIN BROWN
3rd Assistant Director . . . . ADAM BOCKNEK
Trainee Assistant Directors. . . . .

ARIC DUPERE	KIM PALMEN
PATRICK HAGARTY	EDNEY HENDRICKSON
DWIGHT HENDRICKSON	JONATHAN KATZ
KATRINA LEE	NICOLAS LOPEZ
JEFF MUHSOLDT	CRAIG NEWMAN
	JODI TARIO

Canadian Casting. . . . . DIANE KERBEL, C.S.A.

Casting Associate . . . . MICHELLE LEWITT

Casting Assistant. . . . . CRYSTAL PROCTOR
Extras Casting . . . . ZAMERET KLEIMAN
Consultants. . ANGELO DUNDEE   MIKE DELISA
JACK NEWFIELD   PETER HELLER
SUZANNE WASSERMAN
Unit Publicist . . . . LEE ANNE MULDOON
Still Photographer . . . . GEORGE KRAYCHYK
Dialect Coaches . . . . JUDI DICKERSON
DIANE PITBLADO
Boxing Trainers . . BRIAN JAGERSKY DEAN COPKOV
NICK ALACHIOTIS HECTOR ROCA
WAYNE GORDON
Assistant to Mr. Grazer . . . . MIGUEL RAYA
Assistant to Mr. Hallowell . . . . EVA BURKLEY
Assistants to Producers . . . . . . MINDY WEISSMAN
STACIA PETERS
Assistant to Mr. Howard . . . . MELANIE DONKERS
Assistant to Mr. Crowe. . . . . KEITH RODGER
Assistant to Ms. Zellweger . . MEREDITH CHISLETT
Production Assistants . . RAFAEL FERNANDEZ-STOLL
MICHELLE M. ROBESON   RAQUEL ROSE
JEN MARKOWITZ
Physiotherapist to Mr. Crowe . . . . ERROL ALCOTT
Stand-Ins . . DAVID OLIVER   CHRISTINE FULLER
BRAD MOORE   DIRK MCLEAN
Inflatable Extras Supervisor . . . . JOE BIGGINS
Construction Coordinator . . . . . . JIM HALPENNY
Construction Foreman . . . . ROB BONNEY
Assistant Head Carpenter. . . . . KEVIN FORSTNER
Location Leadmen. . . . .

DAVID DICORPO	MIKE BUTT
KEVIN HUGHES	DONAL O'DONOGHUE
	STEVE ROMOLO

Shop Foreman. . . . . BOB NEWMAN
Labor Foremen . . . . BRIAN KELNICK
MIKE NEWTON
SAL LARIZZA
Key Scenic Artists . . . . IAN NELMES
STEPHANIE YARYMOWICH
Head Painters . . . . RANDY ROSS
MARTIN THOMAS
Head Mold Maker. . . . . ANNIE MORIN
Sign Shop Foreman . . . . FRED FITZPATRICK
Key Greensman. . . . . CHRIS DEELEY
Lead Greensman . . . . STEVEN MIDDLEBROOK
Animal Wrangler . . . . RICK PARKER
Transportation Coordinator . . NORMAN HENDERSON
Transportation Captain . . . . JOHN OZOLINS
Driver Co-Captain . . . . PAUL MARSHALL
Head Driver. . . . . STUART HUGHES
Picture Car Coordinator. . . . . SCOTT MAGEE

Picture Car Captain . . . . JOHN HILTZ
Caterer . . . . BY DAVID'S
Chef. . . . . JODIE THORNBER
Set Medic. . . . . STEWART WHITE
Security . . . . MARK CARROLL
DIMAS FREITAS

SECOND UNIT

Second Unit Director . . . . TODD HALLOWELL
Unit Production Manager . . . . . STEVE WAKEFIELD
Production Supervisor . . . . EVA BURKLEY
Production Coordinator . . . . . . ROBIN M. REELIS
Production Assistant . . . . TORI LARSEN
First Assistant Director. . . . . MARK WALLACE
Second Assistant Director . . . . . GEORGE JEFFERY
Third Assistant Director . . . . DAVID COULTER
Director of Photography . . . . GLEN KEENAN
Camera Operator. . . . . PETER LUXFORD
First Assistant Camera . . . . . . ANDREW MEDICKY
Second Assistant Camera . . . MICHAEL MEAGHER
Loader . . . . DAVE McKANE
Script Supervisor. . . . . THANA SPILLIOS
Set Costume Supervisor . . . . . CAROLE COSTELLO
Gaffer . . . . NORM O'HALLORAN
Best Boy Electric . . . . JOHN O'BOYLE
Generator Operator . . . . . . MORGAN CARPENTER
Key Grip . . . . MARK MANCHESTER
Best Boy Grip . . . . WALTER LIPSCOMBE
Dolly Grip . . . . KEN PICKETT
Hair Stylist. . . . . KAROLA DIRNBERGER
Assistant Location Manager . . . MARK McFADDEN
Location P.A. . . . . NEIL WILCOX
Makeup . . . . BURTON LeBLANC
Property Master . . . . GREG PELCHAT
Assistant Prop Master . . . . MICHAEL HUSCHKA
Set Dressers. . . . . CHRIS DEELEY
STEVEN MIDDLEBROOK
Sound Recordist . . . . GLEN GAUTHIER
Boom Operator. . . . . DAVE BELL
Transportation Coordinator . . . . STUART HUGHES
Transportation Captain. . . . . . . ROBERT TENAGLIA
Picture Car Coordinator. . . . . SCOTT MAGEE
Video Assist Operator . . . . . . ANTHONY NOCERA
VFX Concept Artist . . . . JOHN FRASER
Post Production Facility . . . . . . SOUNDTRACK F/T
Post Sound Supervisor . . . . . . STEVE CASTELLANO

Re-Recording Mixers . . . . TOM FLEISCHMAN
BOB CHEFALAS

Supervising Sound Editor. . . . CHIC CICCOLINI III

Add'l. Re-Recording Mixer. . . . . TONY VOLANTE
Dialogue Editors . . . . STAN BOCHNER

DAN KORINTUS
Sound Effects Editors . . . . . . DANIEL PAGAN, MPSE
BRANKA MRKIC-TANA, MPSE
EYTAN MIRSKY
ADR Supervising Editor . . . . DEBORAH WALLACH
ADR Editor . . . . KENNA DOERINGER
Assistant ADR Editor . . . . ANGELA ORGAN
Foley Supervising Editor . . . .
PAM DeMETRUIS THOMAS
Foley Editors . . . . MISSY COHEN
DAVID BARNABY
Assistant Sound Editors . . . . . KATHERINE MILLER
LYNN SABLE
Foley Recorded at . . . . C5, INC.
Foley Artist . . . . MARKO COSTANZO
Foley Engineer . . . . GEORGE A. LARA
ADR Mixer (New York) . . . . DOUG MURRAY
ADR Mixer (Los Angeles) . . . . GREG STEELE
ADR Group Coordinator. . . . . . LYNNE REDDING
Recordists . . . . DAVE BIHLDORFF
DAVE CORCORAN
CARLIE BERGMAN

Executive in Charge of Music for
Universal Pictures . . . . KATHY NELSON
Music Consultant . . . . GEORGE BUDD
Music Editor. . . . . BILL BERNSTEIN
Assistant Music Editor . . . . MICHAEL ZAINER
Music Scoring Mixer . . . . TOMMY VICARI
Orchestra Recorded by . . . . ARMIN STEINER
Recordists. . TOM HARDESTY   TIM LAUBER
ADAM MICKALAK   PATRICK SPAIN
BRIAN DIXON
Orchestration . . . . THOMAS PASATIERI
WILLIAM ELLIOTT
Digital Audio. . . . . JESSE VOCCIA
Music Contractor . . . . LESLIE MORRIS
Music Preparation. . . . . JULIAN BRATOLYUBOV
Temp Music Editor . . . . DAN LIEBERSTEIN
Music Recorded at. . . . . THE VILLAGE
SIGNET SOUND STUDIOS
NEWMAN SCORING STAGE
SONY SCORING STAGE
Mixed at . . . . SIGNET SOUND STUDIOS

Special Visual Effects and Digital Animation by
DIGITAL DOMAIN

Visual Effects Supervisor. . . . . . MARK O. FORKER

VFX Producer . . . . TODD ISROELIT
Computer Graphics Supervisor . . . .
ANDY McGRATH WAISLER

Compositing Supervisor . . . . DARREN M. POE
Digital Production Manager . . . . . . BRIAN PEYATT
Digital Compositors . . . .
    KEVIN BOUCHEZ   DAN COBBETT
    SEAN DEVEREAUX   YANN DORAY
    SCOTT GASTELLU   DAG IVARSOY
    GABRIELLA KALAIZIDIS KEVIN LINGENFELSER
    BRANDON MCNAUGHTON   DEVIN UZAN
               CHRISTOPHER WOOD
Digital Matte Painting Lead . . . . METIN GUNGOR
Digital Matte Painters . . . . MANNIX BENNETT
               DANIEL FAVINI
CG Modeling Lead . . . . MELANIE OKAMURA
CG Effects Animators . . . . TODD BOYCE
               CARLOS D. LEMUS
3D Integration Artist . . . . SOM SHANKAR
Technical Developers . . . . JONAH HALL
               PETER PLEVRITIS
Digital Rotoscope / Paint Artists . . . . JOSH BOLIN
               STEPHEN MITCHELL
VFX Editor . . . . DEBRA WOLFF
Assistant VFX Editor . . . . LINDA RENAUD
Color Grader . . . . TODD SARSFIELD
VFX Production Coordinator . . HEATHER ELISA HILL
Digital FX 2D Coordinator . . . . . BONNIE LEMON
Digital FX 3D Coordinator . . . COLLEEN MURPHY
VFX Production Assistant . . . . . . JAMISON HUBER
VFX Executive Producer . . . . NANCY BERNSTEIN

Visual Effects by
& COMPANY
Visual Effects Supervisor . . . . DAVID ISYOMIN
VFX Executive Producer . . . . CHRIS GELLES
VFX Producer . . . . RICHARD FRIEDLANDER
Compositing Supervisor . . . . GLENN ALLEN
Head of Technology . . . . GREGORY GELLES
Digital Artists . . . . CHRIS BOYCE
               ADAM OSTERFELD

Digital Opticals & Titles . . . . PACIFIC TITLE
Negative Cutter . . . . GARY BURRITT
Color Timer . . . . STEVE BOWEN
Digital Intermediate by . . . . EFILM
Camera Systems . . . . CLAIRMONT
Telecine . . . . DELUXE TORONTO
Grip/Lighting Equipment . . . .
               PRODUCTION SERVICES LTD.

**SOUNDTRACK ON DECCA / UMG
SOUNDTRACKS**

"SHIM-ME-SHA-WABBLE"
Written by Spencer Williams
Performed by Miff Mole and His Molers
Courtesy of Columbia Records
By arrangement with Sony BMG Music Licensing

"CHEER UP, SMILE, NERTZ"
Written by Norman Anthony, Misha Portnoff,
Wesley Portnoff
Performed by Eddie Cantor
with Phil Spitalny's Music
Courtesy of Bright Ventures

"PUT THAT SUN BACK IN THE SKY"
Written by Irving Kahal, Joseph Meyer
Performed by Roane's Pennsylvanians
Courtesy of Bluebird / Novus / RCA Victor
By arrangement with Sony BMG Music Licensing

"HAPPY BIRTHDAY TO YOU"
Written by Mildred J. Hill, Patty S. Hill

"TILLIES DOWNTOWN NOW"
Written by Lawrence (Bud) Freeman
Performed by Bud Freeman and
His Windy City Five
Courtesy of EMI Records
Under License From EMI Film & Television Music

"SOMEDAY SWEETHEART"
Written by John Spikes, Benjamin Spikes

"DON'T BE THAT WAY"
Written by Benny Goodman, Mitchell Parish,
Edgar Sampson

Filmed in part at Toronto Film Studios.

Filmed on location at the Ontario Heritage
Centre, Toronto, Ontario, Canada.

"Dempsey vs. Tunney" by Gustav Rehberger ©
The Estate of Gustav Rehberger, 2004.

Posters courtesy of Circus World.

New York Daily News, L.P. used with permission.

The Filmmakers Gratefully Thank

Madison Square Garden

Jim Roe, Wayne Penford – Maple Leaf Sports & Entertainment Ltd.

Toronto Film and Television Office

The Hudson's Bay Company

1010 WINS Radio

Louis Vuitton Luggage & Leather Goods

American Humane Association monitored the animal action. No animal was harmed in the making of this film. (AHA 00706)

Color by TECHNICOLOR
KODAK Motion Picture Film

DTS®
SDDS
Dolby Digital

ABOUT THE CONTRIBUTORS

The Academy Award®-winning filmmaker **Ron Howard** (Directed by/Produced by) is one of his generation's most popular directors. From the critically acclaimed dramas *A Beautiful Mind* and *Apollo 13* to the hit comedies *Parenthood* and *Splash*, he has created some of Hollywood's most memorable films. He recently earned an Oscar® for Best Director for *A Beautiful Mind*, which also won awards for Best Picture, Best Screenplay, and Best Supporting Actress.

Academy Award®-winning producer **Brian Grazer** (Produced by) has been making movies and television programs for more than 20 years. As both a writer and producer, he has been personally nominated for three Academy Awards®, and in 2002 he won the Best Picture Oscar® for *A Beautiful Mind*. Over the years, Grazer's films and TV shows have been nominated for a total of 39 Oscars® and 42 Emmys. At the same time, his movies have generated more than $11.2 billion in worldwide theatrical, music, and video grosses.

Born in Augusta, Georgia, **Cliff Hollingsworth** (Story by/Screenplay by) grew up in the nearby town of Barnwell, South Carolina. Intent on pursuing his dream of becoming a screenwriter, Hollingsworth moved to Los Angeles. After a few near-miss projects over the years, it was his story idea and screenplay about 1930s boxer Jim Braddock, the "Cinderella Man," that was eventually optioned by Universal. *Cinderella Man* marks Hollingsworth's feature film screenwriting debut.

Akiva Goldsman (Screenplay by) received the highest honors in the film industry, the 2001 Academy Award®, Golden Globe and Writers Guild Award, for his groundbreaking portrayal of schizophrenia in his adaptation of *A Beautiful Mind*. Goldsman's writing credits also include *The Client, Batman Forever, A Time to Kill, Practical Magic,* and *I, Robot*. He is currently working on an adaptation of *The Da Vinci Code*, to be directed by Ron Howard.